Idyllily Wild

By

Sharon L Letson

Michigan ✣ California

ISBN: 979-8-9905086-1-3

sascandapub@gmail.com

Sascanda.org

Cover Design: Shutterstock #**1257481663**

For Lily, who gets to be smart and daring and speak her mind. And for all the women who don't feel brave enough yet to do so.

Chapters

Haven by the Sea

"Lily Jane Wilder! You look frozen through! Come and warm yourself by the fire."

Lily's mother grabbed her hand and pulled her into the sitting room where Mr. Wilder had a fire roaring. "Papa! Move your foot," she demanded as she ushered Lily to his footstool to situate her in front of the fire.

"My Little Idyllily," Papa fussed, "you should not have stayed out so long."

While Mama pulled off her gloves and scarf, Papa worked at her boots. Lily explained through chattering teeth, "I'm sorry, but both the Walkers and Clarks have the fever, and I was obliged to cross to the other side of the village twice with hot soup for them."

"Could no one else go to one while you went to the other?" Mama asked.

"The Spencers work you too hard," Papa scolded. "We should not have given you leave to work for them. We could have managed without the extra pay."

"Papa," Lily frowned. "You know the Spencers are kind and generous, and employ me out of their immense fondness for you. Besides, the other servants are sick," she replied, planting a kiss on his cheek. "Oooh, you are so warm," she said, snuggling in for more.

Papa chuckled and pulled her onto his lap. "Fetch me the quilt, Mama. Let's get our little buttercup warm. And put on the kettle for tea," he called after her.

Lily closed her eyes. She might be almost a grown-up young lady, but she would never be too old to snuggle with her dear Papa.

"Lily?"

Lily startled and her eyes flew open. She was not snuggled in her father's lap. Instead, she was leaning into the willow tree she had climbed into, where she had gone to have a good cry.

"Niece?" Uncle Nael called. Lily swiftly brushed away her tears hoping her Uncle Nael wouldn't see. "Are you well, Niece?"

"Yes, Uncle. Of course," Lily answered, willing her voice to be as cheery as possible. She smiled at him from her perch in the tree.

Uncle Nael was relieved. He had little experience in comforting anyone. Especially one who had lost so much as Lily had.

"Come, return to the garden and sit with me then," he invited as he held out his hand for her to climb down. "It does not befit a young lady of standing to be climbing trees, and I fear for your safety in that one. It has been damaged. I see that Cecilia has set the tea out for us." Lily nodded as she grasped his hand to climb down.

"Mind that broken part. I don't know why you prefer this half-dead tree over all of the trees in my garden," Uncle Nael added.

Lily sighed. Truth be told she wasn't sure herself why she was drawn to the tree which appeared to have been split by a great force. Maybe because it so perfectly mirrored herself. Only half living, holding on to what was now dead with all her might.

"The broken half makes a perfect stair step to that

shaded seat there," she simply said. "And I love to sit by the stream here. It's so peaceful, when I'm feeling lonely for them."

Uncle Nael smiled as she took his arm. "I am fond of that tree myself, which is probably why I've never had it cut down."

"How was it damaged, Uncle?" Lily asked as she took a place on the garden bench while Uncle Nael sought a nearby chair.

Uncle Nael grew quiet and looked thoughtful, before shaking his head. "I have been thinking, Niece," he said, changing the subject. "I worry for you being here all alone with no one your age to socialize with."

"Cecilia is my age," she offered.

Uncle Nael scowled. "We do not socialize with servants!"

"Yes, Uncle. Of course." Lily replied, quietly.

"I'm sorry, Dear One," he said, taking her hand. "I sounded just like my father then. And it made me cringe. I just worry for you," he continued. "You are my ward now and I have a responsibility to you. More than just allowing you to haunt my gardens and fields wearing nothing but black. It has been almost a year. Certainly, we could throw a party and you will allow me to introduce you to my friends. It has done you no good to have no society"

"But Uncle," she protested. "You live here alone, rarely socialize and it doesn't seem to have done you any harm."

Nael laughed. What an imp of a niece he had. But then he quickly sobered. "I am a grumpy old curmudgeon, who desires no one's society but my own," he replied. "But you are a beautiful, young lady, who should be introduced to the society I can provide for you here."

Lily shook her head. "I couldn't bear it, Uncle. Not yet."

Nael thought to press her, but decided against it. Her 'not yet' encouraged him. "Very well. But in time, I hope you will think better of it."

He stood to leave her, but glancing at the sky decided she had better accompany him to the house. "Come dear," he said, offering her his arm. "The weather is turning. Never mind the tea," he scolded as she moved to pick it up. "I'll send Cecilia for it, and I'll have her bring us a fresh pot. This has grown cold."

Lily put down the tray and took her Uncle's arm. She didn't have the heart to tell him that it was not her grief alone that kept her from society. She feared not knowing the rules and that someone would take her for nothing more than a housemaid. At the Spencer's she worked in the kitchen and never went above stairs.

"Uncle, I never thanked you for taking me in," Lily started. "I know Grandfather disowned Mother after she married Father. I didn't expect you to come for me."

"Pshaw, Child. Do you think I would leave you to the generosity of Colonel Spencer when you are my own flesh and blood? The only child of my only sister?"

Lily leaned her head against her Uncle's arm. The childish gesture pleased him. "Your mother was a dear sister to me, and I was heartbroken when she left. If I couldn't be of service to her - she refused to let me help them, due to your father's pride – then I must be allowed to be of service to you."

"Thank you, Uncle."

"I have another thought, Niece," Uncle Nael offered. "Your year of mourning is almost over. You must be tired of wearing black."

"Nay Uncle. I have no interest in new clothes."

"Nonsense Niece. I have engaged the dressmaker to make you a new wardrobe. She will come to take the measurements, but we must go there to pick the fabrics. You will indulge me in this," he directed.

Lily thought for a moment. She must try to be more complying. "Of course, Uncle. If you wish. When must we go?"

Uncle Nael smiled and seized upon Lily's willingness to comply. "On the morrow. After breakfast. The carriage has already been ordered. And mind you pick some ribbons and frills. I will not have my niece dressed plainly."

The man disliked misleading his niece, but he was desperate to think of something to get her out of the house. He was afraid she would find an excuse not to go if he waited. He would have to order the carriage right away and send a message to the dressmaker to expect them.

Lily smiled. Her uncle was a kind man, no matter how gruff he tried to seem. He had planned an outing to the dressmaker and she had agreed. She was nervous about the trip and thought to talk her uncle out of it at breakfast, but she didn't have the chance.

Perhaps he sensed her reluctance, but the moment she sat down he began talking about the time she needed to be ready for the carriage. "And mind you pick some ribbons and frills. I'll not have my niece dressed plainly.

At the dressmaker's it seemed his warning was

needed.

"Niece, what are these?" he asked. "I don't see a lively color in the bunch. Is this gray? And what kind of fabric is this? Cecilia is dressed better than this."

"I'm sorry, Uncle. I didn't want to be extravagant. You have been so kind already."

"Pish. Extravagant you will be. I demand it. It is every fine dress your mother should have worn. What about the blue?"

Lily fingered the blue thoughtfully. It was fine without being insufferable. And it was her father's favorite color. He had often told her that he had named her for the blue lily that grew high in the mountains in a strange village he had visited once called Idyllwild. He fancied the name and thought it fine for a child, but of course his wife shortened it to Lily. But that did not keep him from calling her Idyllily. Idyllily Wild when she was particularly mischievous.

"And the blue ribbon," Uncle added, addressing the dressmaker as he saw that she consented to the fabric.

"Don't make it too fancy. Please Uncle, I would feel conspicuous."

"But not too plain either," Nael directed. "And something sunny, like this yellow."

Lily laughed. "Uncle, I look horrible in yellow. I could never wear it. How about this? What is it called?"

"Periwinkle," the dressmaker offered, taking the fabric and holding it next to Lily's face for Uncle Nael to approve.

He smiled. "Yes, periwinkle is lovely on you. But come, these are all still too plain. You must have some fancy dresses. I intend to hold a ball to show you off."

"Uncle!" Lily exclaimed horrified. "I've never attended a ball in my life! I wouldn't know how to act or what to do. I, I..."

"Peace, Child. Very well, no balls. Until you are ready. But a grumpy old curmudgeon must be allowed a gathering with friends." Lily shot him a look. "A small gathering. With a very few close friends. We'll invite the Spencers," he offered.

Lily laughed. The very thought of the Spencers socializing with their former kitchen maid.

"Come Niece. You said you would indulge me, and it pleases me that you should have some party dresses."

Lily shook her head. She had to yield. "Would this suit?" she asked the dressmaker, holding up a lovely lavender.

The woman nodded. "Paired with this," she said, handing over a delicate fabric with purple and yellow flowers adorning it. "I will make it tasteful, but not overdone."

Lily flushed. The pairing was very pleasing. She nodded and turned away abruptly, looking too intently at some finery that she had no interest in.

She was angry with herself. How could she be so frivolous? Her mother was never frivolous. She was so careful with every penny the family had. And remade her own dresses over as new ones for Lily.

Uncle Nael concluded their business with the dressmaker and appeared at her side. "That's enough for today. I've asked her to make some suitable choices. Is tomorrow week acceptable for the measuring?"

Lily nodded and Nael indicated the same to the

dressmaker.

She was quiet on the road home, and Uncle Nael would not try to make her speak. He simply whispered, "you did well today," as he helped her from the carriage.

"Thank you, Uncle," she whispered back. But alone in her room she could not hold her emotions at bay. She sobbed her grief into her pillow and stayed that way until morning.

A Trysting Tree and a Trunk Full of Shoes

The week until the dressmaker's arrival was uneventful. Uncle Nael realized that he had pushed too hard, and he allowed Lily to wander the gardens and fields unhindered. They seemed to provide her some comfort where he had failed to do so.

But Lily chaffed at his habit of summoning her the moment the weather looked like it might turn stormy.

"Uncle," she protested. "You coddle me. I have my wrap and the breeze feels refreshing."

"Indulge me," he coaxed. "Come sit by the fire with me."

Lily suddenly paled at the memory of her father in his chair by the fire. "It's too warm for a fire," she protested.

"Then play with me at cards."

"I will write a letter and you would do well to do aught more purposeful than playing at cards," she directed.

"You are right, of course. I should find a purpose to my life. Although, I had thought my purpose was to take care of my orphaned niece and be of use to her," he said as he looked over her shoulder.

Lily chided herself. "One game of cards then. But you will have to teach me the rules. I've never played at cards before." Unfortunately for Lily, she found the game confusing and was quite perplexed by her uncle's use of the word 'trump'. Finally, he gave up trying to teach her and let her alone to write her letter.

"Ah, Doctor Samuels is coming," Uncle Nael said as he spied his friend through the window. "I will see if he will play me at cards."

Lily was grateful Uncle Nael had something else to attend to. He could be too attentive, though she knew he meant well. He mourned her parents as well. Mourned the years he missed with his sister and seemed intent on spoiling her in her mother's stead.

"I wonder if there is a purpose I could set him to on my behalf that would keep him from pouring his attentions on me," she thought. She determined to study on it. If she was at home with her parents they would have come up with a scheme. Father was sure to have an idea.

"I must ask him," she thought to herself before she could catch it and remind herself it was impossible.

"Should I send someone to town to post your letter?" Uncle Nael asked. He had returned from his visit with Doctor Samuels who didn't have time for cards.

"Shall we walk to town ourselves, Uncle?" Lily asked.

"Walk?" Nael protested. "It is at least half a mile! And I think it might rain," he said, glancing out the window.

"Come Uncle. Indulge me," Lily said smiling.

"Humph. Is this what it's like to have a conniving, wheedling child, who has wrapped your heart around her finger?" he asked as he allowed himself to be pulled to his feet and his hat and coat to be summoned.

"When is the last time you have walked farther than the garden to fetch me indoors?" Lily scolded. "If I must submit to be pampered and spoiled then so must you."

"Must I?" Uncle Nael asked.

"I insist, Uncle. At least for today. I want to post my letter and I know you will not allow me to walk to town alone. And you will not trust me to one of the servants."

Uncle Nael continued to grumble. "But why not send James? It is much more efficient for him to ride to town. He would be back in a thrice," Uncle Nael said even as they were gaining the road. "It seems so common to walk. Important people do not walk."

"I am common, Uncle. And I am tired of the house and gardens. Let us see what there is to see. For example, have you ever seen that before?" she said, nodding toward a spacious meadow with a perfectly situated tree in the middle. "That tree must hold many secrets."

"Why yes, Niece. It is my meadow and my tree. I often climbed that tree as a boy. I can attest to some of the secrets it holds."

"Truly? How wonderful, Uncle. Then we should go that way," Lily announced, changing direction.

"Go that way? There is no road. And it will add to our journey," Uncle Nael protested, as he followed his niece through the spring grass in the direction of the aforementioned tree.

"I want to hear stories from when you were a boy. And of Mother too. Did she come here with you?"

"Your mother? Why no. Our mother wouldn't allow it. Your mother was being raised to be a lady of society. But I think this may have been their trysting tree."

"Whose?" Lily asked.

"Your parents."

"What is a trysting tree?" she asked.

"Where they met when she was able to slip away. You see, he worked in town and she would wait there until he passed on his way home."

"Father lived near here? Where was his home?" Lily asked, excitedly as they neared the tree.

"I cannot say. I only know that he walked that path below," Uncle Nael replied as they gained the shelter of the tree. "And his house was beyond that hill. Perhaps I could spy it from the branches, though I don't think it would be dignified to climb a tree, even if my niece is partial to the activity. If someone were to see me," he said thoughtfully, as he placed a foot on the tree looking as if he meant to hoist himself up.

Lily placed her hand on his arm. "No Uncle. Do not endanger your dignity. There will be another way for me to see it."

Uncle Nael was thoughtful. "Yes, there is another way. But we must go on horseback. There is no proper road."

"Horseback?" Lily questioned. "Couldn't we walk? It doesn't look far."

"Twice as far as the village, Child, or more. I've never ventured in that direction, and I wouldn't hazard it, not knowing the condition of the footpath."

"I wonder if any of his family still lives about," Lily thought. "He told me of a brother and his parents, my grandparents. I've never met them of course. And we never received any news of them, but he told me stories."

"I doubt they would still be about," Uncle Nael replied. "That area is owned by a landowner named Hanson and he lets out the shacks to the seasonal hands that work his crops. They move on after the harvest. They call it Hanson's Hollow."

"Perhaps they returned," Lily offered.

"Perhaps," Uncle Nael replied. "We could inquire."

"This is a beautiful tree though, Uncle," Lily told him as she caressed a nearby branch. "So many spreading branches. And my parents were here. Thank you for telling me. This will hold a special place in my heart always. When I ache for them, Uncle, may I come here? I feel as if I could talk to them, and they would hear me."

"Not alone, Niece. Promise me that you will not walk this far alone. It would not be seemly," he said sternly.

Lily sighed. "You may come, Uncle, but leave me to myself so I can visit alone."

Uncle Nael looked thoughtful. He did not like walking in general, but he ultimately agreed. "Of course."

"Will you now?" Lily implored. "Just for a moment."

"Of course, Niece," Uncle Nael replied. "I will walk on ahead and wait for you there by that rock. No need to hurry. The sky seems quite clear," he called back as he strode away.

It was several moments before Lily rejoined her Uncle. "Did you mention me?" he teased.

"I told them you were quite a handful," Lily replied. Uncle Nael pretended to be affronted as she took his arm. "And that you miss them too," she said, kissing his cheek.

On the way to town, Uncle Nael continued to tell Lily stories of her mother's childhood and what he knew of her father's courtship of her. She was truly grateful, in this moment, that her Uncle had insisted she come live

19

with him, no matter how apprehensive she was about coming to a place and people she didn't know.

The day the dressmaker was to arrive for her first fitting, Lily was nervous. Would the finished gowns be too fine for her? She was relieved that the dressmaker brought her daughter to help her. The girl was close in age to Lily and put her at ease as she helped her with the underthings.

"These are the prettiest undergarments I've ever owned," Lily exclaimed.

The girl blushed with pride. "I heartily thank ya, Miss."

"Did you make these?" Lily asked, astonished. "They are so fine!"

"Yes, Miss. Mother is training me. I haven't been allowed to do more than the simplest of dresses, but she says my underthings show promise."

"They certainly do!" Lily exclaimed. "You must make one of my dresses. I insist. You choose the trimmings and fittings."

"Truly, Miss?" the girl asked in awe.

"I will ask your mother to allow it, "Lily replied. "She must give you the opportunity to show your skills. No one sees the underthings."

The girl giggled. "Underthings aren't for showing, Miss! They're for wearing."

"Well, I want everyone to see how well you sew. You will rival your mother soon."

"Oh no, Miss. Not for many years yet. But I hope to, someday."

"I'm glad you're pleased with Emmy's sewing, Miss," the dressmaker added as she returned with the first dress. "Arms up," she directed as she and Emmy lowered the dress over Lily's head.

This one had a dark rosy hue, and Lily didn't remember the fabric from her visit to the store. "Your Uncle gave me leave to choose some for you," the dressmaker said, answering her perplexed look. "Look at this against your hair."

"It suits you, Miss," Emmy added. "Truly. It's very becoming."

"It needs to be taken in," her mother declared. "Just a bit tighter here," she said, pulling at the bodice.

"It's a bit revealing," Lily said, with concern.

"Emmy, fetch the cream scarf," the dressmaker directed. "There that suits," she declared as she added it. "And it is more discrete."

"Are they all this low?" Lily asked.

"Your Uncle directed me to make them in the latest style. And the latest style demands low necklines."

"I'm not sure Uncle would have asked it if he had seen the latest style," Lily mused. "And I don't think Uncle would approve of my bosoms appearing to jump from the dress."

"They are your gowns, Miss. I will make them however you like," the dressmaker replied.

"I like Emmy's gown," Lily declared. "Favor me by making them as if Emmy was the one who was to wear them."

The dressmaker smiled. "You are very sensible, Miss. With your permission we'll return tomorrow. And I'll send the matching fabrics to the Milliner's to begin your bonnets."

"Bonnets?" Lily asked. "I have only one head. How

many bonnets do I need?"

"One for each dress, Miss," Emmy replied.

"One for each dress?" Lily exclaimed.

"And shoes to match," Emmy added.

"Do you have a bonnet for every dress you own, Emmy, and a pair of shoes too?"

"Well, not I, Miss. But fancy ladies do."

"Two bonnets would be more suitable. One for every day and one for fancy. The same goes for shoes. Uncle may dress me up if he likes, but he will not make me so frivolous as to need more than two bonnets and two pairs of shoes."

Emmy giggled at this speech. "Very well," the dressmaker said, shooting her daughter a disapproving look, "but the same bonnet would not look well with every fancy dress your Uncle has ordered."

"How many fancy dresses did Uncle order?" Lily asked, alarmed. "I thought we settled on the blue and the periwinkle for fancy and three or four serviceable dresses for everyday. That is already almost as many dresses as there are days in the week. How many dresses does a body need?"

"I believe your Uncle said you were 'indulging him'," the dressmaker slyly said as they helped Lily off with the rose colored dress.

Lily sighed. She should not be ungrateful. "Very well, have the bonnets made. But I draw the line at shoes."

Lily's benevolent spirit toward her Uncle's generosity lasted until the day the dresses arrived. As trunk after trunk was carried in, she began to panic.

"What have you done, Uncle?" she whispered. "It's

too…, too extravagant!" And as the dresses were unpacked and displayed she added, "There are too many!"

"I say there are too few," Uncle Nael countered. "How many years are you?"

"Nearly 20, Uncle. But what has that to do with it?"

"Almost 20 missed years. Missed birthdays, where I was not allowed to dote on my niece. And now you are my only living relation."

Lily softened, but was not yet mastered. "But where are the everyday dresses? I can't parade around like this on a walk to town!"

"The everyday dresses are here, Miss," Emmy directed. "In this trunk. Mother allowed me to take charge of these myself," she said proudly.

"Thank you, Emmy," Lily gasped. "You have saved me." But as the dresses were unpacked, Lily didn't have the heart to tell her that these would have done for fancy back home.

After the trunks were moved up to her rooms, Lily sat next to her uncle. "Uncle," she began softly, thinking to scold him.

"Do you remember when you visited here?" Uncle Nael interrupted.

"Visited here? I was here?" she asked, surprised.

"No, of course you don't remember. You were too young. But I remember it vividly. It is one of my happiest memories," he said thoughtfully.

"When was I here, Uncle? Why do I not remember this?" Lily asked.

"You were running through the garden, willing me

23

to chase you. And you squealed with delight every time I did. Running on those chubby little legs. Your curls bouncing in the sunshine."

Lily smiled at the story. In her memory it had been Father who was chasing her.

"You were afraid of me at first," Uncle continued. "Your mother said it was because I wore a beard and your father was clean shaven. But you warmed to me eventually."

Lily was astonished. "Why did we not return? Why only that one visit? I had grandparents and an uncle. Why was I not allowed to know them, or you?" Lily wondered.

"The war," Uncle Nael sighed. "Your father went to fight and returned wounded. Your mother said it would pain him too much to ride this far with only his one leg."

"But you could have come to us? Why did you not do so?" Lily asked.

Uncle Nael smiled wryly. "Pride, I guess. It was left to me to uphold the honor of the Mildenhall name. And Father prevented it. I could have defied him, I suppose. But I thought he must be right and so I acquiesced. And now..."

"Uncle."

"Nay, let's not be melancholy on this fine day. I promised you a ride. Go and change. I'll have no more of that black."

"Uncle."

"I insist. The navy will do for a start. Or the burgundy. Just not black. You have plenty to choose from."

Lily laughed. "Yes, it will take a year to wear all those dresses. Very well. The burgundy is suitable for

24

riding. However, you have neglected an item of importance."

"What have I neglected? I ordered everything, including riding boots," Uncle Nael blustered.

"Uncle, I have never ridden a horse in my life. I don't know how," Lily protested.

"Oh, is that all," Uncle Nael laughed. "That is easily remedied. I'll have James saddle my gentlest mare. She will follow my horse. You won't even need to direct her. Though, I see you will have to have lessons. A proper lady should be an accomplished rider. Now, go and change."

Lily nodded and moved towards the stairs. " I'm sure you'll find the riding boots in the trunk with the other shoes," he called after her.

Lily whirled. "A trunk? Full of shoes? Uncle!"

A Ride and A Surprise

Cecilia was soon put to work helping Lily dress. There were pulls, stays, and buttons that Lily could not reach. "No wonder rich women have ladies' maids," she mused. "It is impossible to dress one's self."

"May I do your hair, Miss?" Cecilia asked her once the dress was accomplished.

"My hair?" Lily asked, touching her brown curls. "What is wrong with my hair?"

"Most ladies wear their hair up," Cecilia offered. "I can arrange it like so with some curls in front and secured in back in case you have occasion to remove your bonnet."

Lily was thoughtful. She liked her hair down. Father had never wanted her to wear it up. He said that the moment she wore her hair up, she would cease being his little girl and he couldn't bear it. "Just secure it with a ribbon so it doesn't fly about, Cecilia," she finally conceded.

"Yes, Miss," Cecilia replied.

Uncle seemed pleased when she descended the stairs. "You look well, young lady. Will you take my arm?"

Lily smiled at her Uncle's formality. "I will not disgrace you then?" she asked.

"Hardly," he replied. "You could never disgrace me. The color is pleasing. But I am glad you chose to leave your hair down. I could not bear you transforming into a grown-up woman all at once. Someone may wish to steal you from me."

Lily laughed. "Hardly, Uncle. I am still a child after all and will need quite looking after."

Lily took her Uncle's arm and they proceeded out of doors to where the horses were waiting. The brown mare looked gentle enough, but Lily wondered how she was to mount her.

"You stand upon the box, Dear," her Uncle offered, "and place your foot here in the stirrup."

"Now what," Lily asked after that was accomplished.

"Well, grab here and you pull yourself upon the seat," her uncle instructed.

Lily leaned over the horse and twisted herself into a sitting position, but she had to take her foot out of the stirrup to do so. "This doesn't seem right, Uncle. I am sidewise."

"Yes, of course, ladies do it differently," Uncle Nael mused. "Bring your knee into this notch and then your other foot can go back into the stirrup. It's called sidesaddle."

"It is uncomfortable," Lily countered.

"You will grow used to it. Proper ladies always ride sidesaddle. Now take the reins in your hands."

"How do I hold on if I have to hold these?" Lily asked, startling as the mare began to move under her, shifting her weight.

"Hold on with one hand and hold the reins with the other until you grow more comfortable. And mind you don't let the reins go. She could trip on them and injure you and herself. Or worse yet, she'll go to eating grass and stop walking altogether. She's a touch lazy."

Lily found the instructions dizzying as they set out. She sat stiff in the seat and held the reins so tightly she lost the feeling in her fingers.

"Relax, Niece," Uncle Nael said as they plodded along. "You will not fall off and if you do the ground is soft and your dress plentiful. It will cushion your fall."

"Uncle, do not make me laugh," Lily protested. "Or I will lose my grip."

"The horse knows what she is doing," he instructed. "She knows how to keep you safe."

"She does?" Lily wondered. "How does she know that?"

"Horses are very intelligent creatures," Uncle Nael replied.

"What is her name?" Lily asked.

"Whose name? The horse?" Uncle Nael asked with surprise. "Well, it is Molly. Called so after an old nanny I had once. I could never get her moving either," he chuckled.

Lily smiled, but would not let herself laugh at the joke. "So, Molly," she said. "Uncle says you'll keep me safe? Is it so?"

Uncle Nael smiled. "She says to lower your hands and stop sitting stiff as a board."

"You speak horse, do you?" Lily asked, grinning.

"Feel the horse move," Uncle Nael instructed. "Move with her. She has a rhythm and you will do better if you match it."

Lily willed herself to relax. She closed her eyes and lowered her hands. She could feel what Uncle meant. It was a steady rolling and swaying. "I think I see, Uncle. Am I doing it now?"

"Better, Dear," he advised. "You have kept your seat well. But here we must leave the road. No, do not stiffen up," he cautioned as he saw her body tense with fear. "It's only that the path may not be smooth. If there's a root or a hole, you must keep vigilant that she doesn't trip and jolt you off."

Lily watched the path so vigilantly that she didn't notice when her uncle had pulled his horse to a stop. "What is the matter, Uncle?" she asked as Molly followed suit.

"I wanted you to look up, Niece." Uncle Nael told her. "I thought you would like to see this."

Lily looked around. The green meadow fell away at their feet and the downward track was full of every manner of wildflowers. "Oh!" she gasped. "And the scent!" she said, breathing deeply.

Uncle Nael smiled. "And the houses beyond. That is what I meant you to see. Somewhere among those is the childhood home of your father."

"Oh Uncle!" she gasped again. "They are so quaint."

"Quaint?" he countered. "I would more say in need of fresh paint and carpentry."

"May we go down?" Lily asked.

"You've ridden a good deal already for your first time," Uncle Nael replied. "I think we should start back."

"No, Uncle! Look," Lily said, pointing to the nearest house. "I see someone there. Let's go down and see if he knows aught of my father."

Lily nudged Molly, but she only looked at her. "Very well, Niece. If you are determined and I can see you are," Uncle Nael said, nudging his horse forward so that Molly would follow. "Let us go down."

"Do you know anything of the people there, Uncle," Lily asked. "It is not a far ride from your house?"

29

"No," he replied. "I am not acquainted with anyone from this area. It is beyond the bounds of my land. And they are not often associated with the town. There has been no reason for our paths to cross."

"Then we shall have to inquire," Lily replied. "Sir," she called as they drew close.

The old man looked up slowly and stared at Lily, making her uncomfortable. "Sir?" Uncle Nael questioned. "Are you well?"

Without a word the man turned and disappeared inside. As they waited atop their horses wondering what to do next, a younger man came to the door and slowly opened it. He too stared at Lily as he stood upon the porch.

"Sir," Lily began timidly. She was vexed by the staring, but determined to know if they were acquainted with her father. "Do you know a man named William Wilder?" she asked.

"Aye," the man acknowledged. "You better come in then."

Lily was thoroughly confused but thought they had better since the man said nothing else. "Should we, Uncle?" she whispered since he did not dismount.

"Yes," he said slowly lowering himself. "I believe we had better." He tied his horse and Molly to a rail and lifted Lily from her seat.

She held onto her uncle a little longer than necessary for her to find her feet. "I believe my foot has fallen asleep," she whispered, keeping her eye on the man on the porch.

"Stamp it a few times," he advised. "And hold my arm tightly until you are sure of yourself."

They walked toward the house together. The old man had returned at the door, which he held open for the pair to pass. They were ushered into a sitting room where a woman sat doing needlework in front of a window with the sun warming her.

"She's here, Mama," the younger man said, kneeling down to speak to the old woman.

The woman turned her face toward the pair. Lily was startled by her loveliness. Her hair was white and her skin wrinkled. But she was lovely.

"I have seen that face before," said Uncle Nael.

"Where?" whispered Lily.

"It is your face," he replied.

Lily took a seat across from the woman who had let her stitching fall to her lap. "Are you? My grandmother?" she asked.

The woman nodded. "She don't speak none," the younger man said. "Stroke the doctor called it. "But she understands your words."

"Then that means you are my uncle?" Lily asked. "And grandfather?" to the older man.

The men nodded. The older man took her hand and kissed it. His eyes were wet with tears.

"You were a wee child when we last saw ya," he told her.

Lily looked at them in amazement. "Well, you all seem to know who I am. Please tell me about you. My father told me some stories, but I am quite bewildered at finding you here."

"Your father didn't mention aught of us?" the younger man asked. "Shame it was then. Shame at his upbringing."

"Nay," the older man countered. "It was his anger at us forbidding him from squiring after that fancy girl from the big house."

"My mother?" Lily asked.

"She was a beauty," the younger man said, nodding. "I be Percy," he said, holding out his hand. "This be my father, William the first. You see, your father was William the second. And mother here is Rosana."

"Such a lovely name," Lily said, taking his hand absently, while staring at the woman. "Rosana."

Suddenly there was a clamor on the porch and a group of children burst through the door. "Hush children," a woman said, following them in. "Cain't you see there be company?"

"Millie, come see who it is," Percy called.

The troop entered and silently stood before Lily. No one paid any attention to Uncle Nael.

"What's your name?" a little blond girl asked Lily, reaching out to touch her curls.

"Lily Wilder. What's yours?"

The girl smiled. "Maggie. I'm Wilder too. Ain't I, Mama?" she queried.

"Aye," Percy said. "That un's Maggie. This here be Cecil, Tommy, and Carl. The little one there is Hazel Grace and the big un holding her is our Luella. She looks pert near your age."

"I am pleased to meet all of you," Lily said with a slight tilt of her head. They curtsied awkwardly in return and huddled around their mama who seemed intent on bustling them out of the room.

"Stay Luella," her father commanded. "I'd like ya to get to know yar cousin." The girl shyly moved to her father.

"Come and sit by me," Lily invited, making room on the settee for her. The girl acquiesced, but like the others did not speak. She simply stared until Millie returned without the children.

"Well, so you're Lily," the portly woman began. "I ain't heard naught but you and your folks since I joined this family."

"You have me at a disadvantage, Ma'am," Lily explained. "I only remember father mentioning a brother and his parents. Nothing like all of this."

"Brother William left us before Millie and me got wed," Percy offered.

"And your fancy gent there? Who be he?" Millie asked snidely.

Uncle Nael rose and bowed to the room. "Forgive me for not introducing myself," he began.

Millie snorted at the demonstration.

"My name is Charles Nael Mildenhall," he continued, ignoring the snort. "I am Lily's uncle and guardian."

"Guardyan?" Millie queried. "What's that mean?"

"It means my William is dead," her father-in-law replied, wiping his eyes. "I should have knowed it. He would uv forgive us and returned before now if it wasn't so."

"You've had no word in all this time?" Lily asked.

"He sent letters," Percy said, rising to pull a bundle from a drawer and handing them to her. "Naught for a few years."

"These aren't opened," Lily asked, perplexed, casting about the room until Uncle Nael caught her eye.

"Oh," she said, realizing what it meant. "You can't read? None of you?"

"Luella can, some," Millie replied. "She's had some learnen. But not enough to decipher those. I think it's your Mam's hand. From what I hear, William couldn't read or write much."

Lily was shocked by this revelation. Of course, her father could read and write! Couldn't he? She was trying to think of a time that her father read something to her or wrote a note, but she couldn't.

"Maybe you could read them to us sometime," Lily's grandfather asked. "I've always wanted to know what his words were."

"Oh of course, Grandfather," Lily gushed. "I would love to hear them myself."

"You will come again?" Luella asked shyly.

"Of course," Lily assured her. "It is not far by horse. But I am not very experienced at riding, so I am dependent on my Uncle's kindness to accompany me."

"Is yar Mam dead too?" Millie asked. "Is that what guardyan means? You ain't got no folks no more?"

Uncle Nael looked affronted, but Millie didn't notice. "Yes, Aunt. May I call you Aunt?" Lily said, intercepting Uncle Nael's look. "My parents died last year, and Uncle Nael was so kind as to have me come and live with him."

"You been livin' in that fancy house for a year and they didn't tell ya about us?" Millie scowled.

"Uncle Nael did not know!" Lily protested, shooting a questioning look at her uncle.

"His folks knowed it," Lily's grandfather said. "I went there to beg 'em to tell me where I could find my

34

boy.

I meant to see him if I could do it, but they just drove me from the door."

Lily looked at Uncle Nael, puzzled by this pronouncement. "My parents died several years ago," Uncle Nael offered. "They didn't share any of this with me. I only knew William used to live in this area. I thought his people had moved on long ago. Following the harvest, as was his way when he courted my sister."

"We returned every spring," Percy explained. "My parents said he would not know where to find us if we left. After Mama's stroke, we stayed put."

"We waited all this time, and now we know he will not come," Lily's grandfather added. "But the child has come," he said, patting her hand. "And she will come again. She has said she will."

"Yes, Grandfather," Lily assured him. "I will come again."

Uncle Nael rose. "I'm sorry, Niece, but the weather seems to be turning. I would like to reach home before it rains. We have already been gone longer than planned."

Lily was reluctant to leave, but complied with her uncle's request. "I will come again, Grandmother. I promise. I'll plan a day when I can stay longer."

"We will send word so that you know to expect us," Uncle Nael added, ushering Lily out the door.

The family gathered on the porch to watch them leave, which was disconcerting for Lily who wasn't sure how she was to mount Molly without the box to help her. Fortunately, Percy saw her predicament and offered his knee as a step while Uncle Nael held Molly's head.

Lily tried to seat herself without letting on what a

35

novice she was at riding. Fortunately, the dress mostly covered her clumsiness.

The ride home was filled with her amazement at finding a house full of unknown relatives. She couldn't fathom why her parents rarely spoke of either of their childhood homes and families. She knew it was her father's injury that prevented them from traveling so far, but why weren't there more stories? "Did they think they were protecting me," she mused. "But from what?"

The questions continued throughout the day and through the evening meal where Nael decided to finally interrupt. "Niece, you came from society *and* poverty and your parents ended somewhere in the middle. Is it not possible that to acknowledge either would endanger the path they chose for themselves? I know my parents would have interfered, often interfered. They liked to direct people's lives."

"But these people weren't like that," Lily protested. "They were..."

"Common," Uncle Nael offered.

"I was going to say simple," Lily countered, somewhat annoyed. It was hard getting used to her uncle's way of elevating himself above those that Lily felt a kinship to. "They just wanted to be a part of our lives."

"They had the letters. They could have gotten someone to read them and to write a reply," Uncle Nael said. His argument seemed reasonable and it silenced Lily long enough for her to contemplate her plate.

"Maybe there was no one they could ask," Lily wondered. "It is a fair walk to town and I saw only shacks nearby. And you said the people there 'followed the harvest'? Is that what you said?"

"Yes, that seems reasonable," Uncle Nael agreed. "If the residents there are transitory, and they had little contact with the town."

"And your parents drove him from the door," Lily added. "Maybe they asked but were rebuffed." She thought for a moment. "But the vicar would have readily done it," she said, frowning.

They sat in silence for a moment, thinking. "There was no vicarage!" they both said at once.

Lily frowned. "No vicarage and no school! Who cares for these people? Do the landlords provide them nothing?

"The landowners are only interested in workers to tend their crops," Uncle Nael replied. "They do not give much thought beyond the work they provide.

"And you, Uncle? Do you hire people like these to tend your fields?" Lily asked.

Uncle Nael was thoughtful. "Yes. But I've never asked who my overseer hires. I leave it to his hands to manage the fields. It's what I pay him for."

"But Uncle! No learning and no preaching. How is anyone to better themselves?"

New Friends

"Mama, who are these people?" Lily asked as she sat on her Mama's lap playing with her locket. She loved making it open and closing it back up again.

"Hmm? Those are my parents, Lovey," Mama said, absently.

"Where are they?" Lily asked. "Why do we not see them?"

"They live far away. Farther away than Papa can travel on his bad leg," Mama replied.

"Will they come here?" Lily asked.

"No, my love," Papa said from his chair. "Go and get your book. I want to hear you read to me."

"Do you have little drawings like Mama does?" Lily asked her father as she brought him her new story book and snuggled up beside him in his chair.

"No, Idyllily. What does this say?" he said pointing to the cover of her book.

"Ffflowers?" Lily said, uncertainly.

"Keep going," her father encouraged.

"Flowers for Mother," Lily read, slowly. "Why don't you have pictures, Papa? Like Mama does."

"It takes money, Dear, to hire an artist to capture a person's likeness," Papa answered. "If I had money, I would hire someone to take your mother's likeness. And then I would wear her around my neck," he teased.

"Papa!" Lily declared. "Don't be a goose. You can't wear Mama around your neck," she said laughing. Then her tone became serious, "If you don't have money, does that mean we are poor?"

"Oh no, my Idyllily. We are not poor. We have all

38

we need," Papa said, squeezing her and smiling at
Mama."

Lily climbed up on her father's lap. "But we don't
need to have Mama hanging from a chain around your
neck, do we? 'Cause she's right here!"

Lily fingered the locket she wore. Uncle had
favored her with a miniature of her mother to put inside,
but she had none of her father. Her heart ached for them
both.

"Uncle, when are we to begin my riding lessons?"
Lily asked at breakfast. "I would like to return to visit my
newfound relations. And we must plan to stay longer this
time."

Uncle Nael smiled. "I have engaged someone to
come starting this very afternoon," he replied. "If you
practice every day, it shouldn't take you long to feel more
comfortable in the saddle."

"Thank you, Uncle!" Lily gushed. "I'm so anxious
to keep my promise and return."

"But I have a thought, Niece," Uncle Nael
continued.

"What are you thinking of now, Uncle?" Lily asked.

"I think you need a proper horse," he replied.

"Uncle, there is nothing wrong with Molly. You
must not spoil me," Lily protested.

"Molly is old and stubborn. And after you learn to
ride properly, you may decide to venture out on your
own. Molly will only follow another horse. She's safe for a
rider who is unfamiliar with horses, but you'll want one
that will go where you choose to go."

Lily could not counter her Uncle's logic, especially
since he mentioned allowing Lily to ride out on her own.

"Will I begin on Molly or a different horse?"

"Well, if you will indulge me and take a carriage ride with me today, we'll go and choose a suitable horse for you. I've asked the breeder to pick out some settled horses that are suitable for a beginning rider."

Lily felt she should protest. Her Uncle was too extravagant with her, but the thought of being able to have the independence of going for a ride on her own was more than she could overcome. "Thank you, Uncle," was all she would venture to say.

At the breeders there were several horses brought into the corral for her to look at, but she had no idea how to choose a horse. They all seemed so much taller than Molly. She thought she would be frightened to sit atop something so big. "Don't you have anything smaller?" she asked.

Uncle Nael nodded to the breeder to do as his niece wished. "I told him you wouldn't want one of those, but he insisted on showing them to you. He is used to fancy ladies who want fancy horses."

The breeder brought in a new group of horses. Lily was happy to see that there were a few that were shorter like Molly. But she still was unsure how to know which one would be good for her.

"Open your parasol," Uncle Nael asked her.

"My parasol?" Lily asked.

"Go on, you'll see," Uncle Nael told her.

Lily did as he asked and opened her parasol. Then she understood as 2 of the horses startled and Uncle Nael told the breeder to take them away.

"Oh!" she cried. She couldn't imagine being atop an animal like that and to have them startle. She'd surely fall off. Then she laughed as her uncle began waving his coat at them. Again, some of them startled and Uncle Nael had them taken away.

"Go to the fence and see which one of them likes you," he instructed Lily.

"Likes me?" she asked. "How will I know if a horse likes me?" she wondered.

"Just go to the fence and we'll see how they react," Uncle Nael instructed.

Lily did as she was asked and walked toward the fence. The horses picked up their heads and watched her. One of them laid her ears back and Uncle Nael immediately had that one dismissed.

Lily was startled by the horses coming to the fence to investigate her. "What do I do, Uncle?" she asked.

"Pat them," Uncle Nael directed. "See if they like it.

"Pat them?"

"Yes, try scratching them on the neck and see if they react if you touch their ears."

Lily was hesitant, but she found that some of the animals liked the scratching and stretched out their necks to get more. Uncle dismissed any that didn't like their ears touched. One in particular seemed very interested in Lily and came and sniffed at her.

"Send the others out, we'd like to see this one," Uncle Nael directed. Once that was done, he opened the gate and ushered Lily into the pen. He walked all the way around the horse and bid Lily to do the same.

"What am I doing, Uncle?" Lily asked.

"You are seeing if the horse reacts to the rustling of your dress," he replied. But the horse did nothing except watch the pair with interest.

41

When they left the pen, the horse followed them to the fence and stretched out her neck for more scratches. "I think this one likes me," Lily whispered.

"And do you like her?" Uncle Nael asked.

"Yes, I think I do," Lily replied. "What is her name?"

"If she is yours, you may choose her name," Uncle Nael replied.

Lily marveled. She had never named another creature before. She would have to think hard to give the animal a proper name.

"Are you satisfied?" Uncle Nael asked.

"Yes," Lily replied. "I like her."

"Good, we'll have her brought to the house this afternoon for your first lesson," Uncle Nael replied.

Lily was quiet on the ride home. Uncle Nael thought she might regret purchasing the horse, but he knew better than to interrupt her thoughts.

Finally, she spoke, "Uncle Nael, how do you name something? I can't think of anything. I don't know how to do it."

"Oh Niece! I thought you were displeased. I was sure your next statement was to chide me for spoiling you," Uncle Nael laughed.

"Well, you do spoil me terribly, Uncle Nael. But I will forgive you in this case when I'm allowed to ride out from the house alone. On occasion," she added when she saw the disapproval on her uncle's face.

"Very well," he replied. "I did promise you some independence when you learned to ride. I am sure you will hold me to it."

"Yes, Uncle. I can be very determined when I have

a mind to be. But you must help me. I don't know how to choose a name."

"To choose a name?" Uncle Nael asked. "Well, I guess I think of what the animal reminds me of. Like Molly, I told you she was named for an old nanny. She reminds me of her."

"Someone she reminds me of?" Lily puzzled.

"Or something. A flower or a tree." Uncle Nael added.

"A tree?" Lily asked puzzled. "Like elm or maple?"

"Willow," Uncle Nael. "Like my horse. She reminds me of a willow tree. With her long legs and the graceful way she walks."

"Something or someone she reminds me of," Lily said thoughtfully. "It may take me some time to think of something. I will need to get to know her first."

Uncle Nael laughed. "Get to know her? A horse?"

"Is that silly?" Lily replied, laughing herself.

"No, I expect not," Uncle Nael said. "I usually go with my first impression of an animal, but sometimes that turns out to be wrong."

When the horse arrived in the afternoon, Lily spent some time with it in the corral. The animal was very affectionate and came over often for scratches and pets, but then would run away and trot around exploring her new environment.

But even during the lesson that afternoon Lily couldn't stop thinking about what to name her. Her coat was silky and soft. "Sophie?" she thought. "Cinnamon? Ginger? Thinking of the horse's color. She was so distracted she was almost unseated."

"Not like that, Miss," the trainer scolded. "You will

43

lose your seat. You must be the master of the horse, not let her take you where she wants to go. And never let her eat grass when she has her bridle on," he said, pulling the horse's head up. The horse reached for his cap and pulled it off his head, in protest.

Lily laughed at the man's indignation, especially since the removal of his cap showed his bald head, which he was quite embarrassed by in the presence of the young lady. "You are a bit of a scamp," she said to the horse. "We are quite well matched in that way."

"Have you thought of a name," Uncle Nael asked over supper.

"I think so," Lily replied. "But I want to think on it for a few days until I'm sure."

Uncle Nael nodded. "And your lesson? How did it go?" he asked.

"We only practiced within the park. I think I did well, but there are so many things to remember at the same time."

"It will come," Uncle Nael said. "You and the horse must learn each other's ways. Become comfortable with each other."

"I will try, Uncle," Lily replied. "I really want to learn."

Lily's riding lessons continued to proceed well, and she was feeling much more comfortable on her new horse. She hoped she'd be able to ride back to her grandparents' house soon and meant to ask Uncle Nael about it, but he did not come down to breakfast.

"Is my uncle ill?" Lily asked Matilda, the kitchen maid who brought her meal.

"No, Miss," the servant replied. "He was

summoned early. T'was urgent, the boy said, so he rode out right away."

Lily was surprised. Meals with her uncle had become familiar and comforting. To suddenly be left alone in the large room brought back unwelcome feelings of grief. She could not eat and pushed the plate away. "Take it away Matilda," she demanded.

"Miss? Are you ill?"

Lily shook her head and pushed back from the table. "Take it away," she repeated. She fled out of doors and made her way to the corral. Her horse came to the fence to whinny at her and see if she had a treat.

"Nothing today, Dearheart," Lily told the horse as she stroked her nose. The horse set her head on Lily's shoulder, in what seemed to her, very much like a hug. Lily leaned in and stroked her neck. "What a good girl you are," Lily whispered. "When there is no one else, you will be here."

"Oh, there you are Niece!" Uncle Nael called, startling Lily. "I'm glad to see you and that horse have made friends. What have you decided to call her?"

"You startled me, Uncle," Lily said, turning toward him. "Why weren't you at breakfast?"

"Oh, didn't Matilda tell you," Uncle Nael replied, concerned that the servant hadn't communicated his message, "I will take her to task."

"No, don't do that, Uncle," Lily protested. "She told me. I just didn't like being alone. It felt so…, lonely."

"Oh, Dear One," Uncle Nael said leaning in to kiss her forehead. "How thoughtless of me. Doctor Samuels sent for me. Said it was urgent. I should have directed Matilda to take your breakfast to your room

45

instead of leaving you to eat in that big empty dining room alone. I couldn't stand that room after my parents died. I had taken to having my meals beside the fire in the study until you came."

"Thank you for understanding, Uncle," Lily said, giving him a squeeze.

"And the horse? What is her name?" Uncle Nael asked motioning toward the horse who was sniffing at his pocket, hoping for a treat.

Lily inhaled and braced herself. She wasn't sure how her Uncle would react. "Bronnie," she declared.

"Bronnie?" Uncle Nael asked, growing quiet.

"Short for Bronwyn. You said to name her after something or someone she reminds me of and with her coloring, mischievousness, and kind nature, she reminds me of mother."

"Bronnie," Uncle said thoughtfully. "It suits her," he said, scratching the horse's neck. "Bronnie. You keep this girl safe," he told the horse.

Lily smiled. "She will. My riding has already improved considerably. I'm ready for that ride back to see my grandparents that you promised me."

"Soon. Well, come to the house," Uncle Nael instructed. "I've missed my breakfast and I'm hungry. And I suspect you are too."

Lily returned to the house with her uncle, and while their meal was reprepared, Lily caught up on the news. "So, what was so urgent that you had to ride out before breakfast?" she asked her uncle.

"I'm not sure it was urgent," Uncle Nael replied. "Only that Doctor Samuels thought it was urgent. His sister and her children are coming to stay, and he was up half the night worrying about it. His nerves are not what they should be for a man of the medical profession."

"Why should he worry about family coming to visit?" Lily asked.

"Exactly," Uncle Nael replied. "That is what I told him, but he reminded me of how nervous I was before you arrived."

"How is that the same?" Lily asked. "You have no children of your own and suddenly you had someone to be responsible for. Of course, you were nervous. You did not know me, and I did not know you."

"The sister's husband has died, and she is moving her family there to stay with him. He feels responsible, the same I felt for you. How could I begin to take the place of a father you loved so dearly? And she has three children."

"What was your advice?" Lily asked, smiling.

"I advised him to be kind and patient," Uncle Nael replied. "And I reminded him that they still have their mother, while you lost both your parents. I also reminded him that you still feel the loss very keenly, as do I, having lost my only sister from the fever that afflicted her, when he still has his."

Lily sighed. "What a pair we are, Uncle," she said. "Both lost in our grief trying to find ourselves again."

Uncle Nael smiled. "I also obligated us for a visit to welcome them to the region. There is a daughter near your age. I thought it would do you both good."

"Oh yes, Uncle," Lily replied. "I hope we shall be good friends."

Grand Plans

The visit the next day went well. Lily thought the daughter was sweet-tempered, though she found the younger brothers a bit spoiled. Their father was the one who took the boys in-hand and without him the mother seemed to have no idea of how to curb their boyish enthusiasm for all outdoors and tormenting their sister. That task now fell to Doctor Samuels, who was completely unprepared for it.

Lily promised to visit regularly. She understood the girl's need to talk about her father and wander the woods and gardens in search of solace.

But first she had another promised visit to make that she felt was overdue. At dinner she begged her Uncle to send word to her grandparents that she would visit on the morrow. He agreed only on condition that he be allowed to ride with her as he didn't feel she was ready to ride out alone. She had not mastered mounting, and should she lose her seat, she would not be able to regain the horse and would have to walk.

Lily had more confidence in her riding abilities, but she felt her Uncle's concern had more to do with her riding to Hanson's Hollow alone. He did not trust the type of people she could find there.

But he had agreed, and the next day they rode out and brought a picnic lunch to share. Aunt Millie refused to take part in any 'vittles from a fancy kitchen' that would make her beholden, but Luella and Lily spread a blanket by the stream and the children joined them.

Out of sight of the grown-ups Luella was much more talkative. Lily admired the way Luella took charge

48

of her brothers and sisters and she felt comfortable with her cousin in a way that seemed impossible with anyone at Uncle Nael's house where she had to be proper all the time. Lily even removed her shoes and stockings so she could play in the stream with the children.

When the group traipsed back into the house, Uncle Nael gave her a disapproving look and Luella hustled her off into a side room so she could put herself in order. When she returned, her grandfather spoke.

"I'm pleased ya remembered yar promise and come again," he said. "And it brightens my heart to see how ya and yar cousins take to each other."

Lily smiled as she held tightly to Luella's hand. "I am fond of them, Grandfather. They are sweet children," she replied.

Her grandfather nodded and wiped at his eyes. "Will ya keep the other part of your promise now and read some of the letters that yar father sent to us?"

"Of course, Grandfather!" Lily exclaimed, chiding herself for forgetting. "I am as eager as you are to hear what they contain."

Uncle Percy retrieved the letters and handed them to Lily. She thought it would be best to read them in order, so she retrieved the oldest one first. She noticed right away that they were penned in her mother's hand, but the words were as if her father were speaking.

"Dear Mother and Father," she began. "The journey home was long, and I am bone tired. I have tucked our dearest Lily into bed and planted an extra kiss on her head for you as I knew you would want. I noted when we were there, how much she takes after you, Mother, excepting the brown curls which my wife tells me come from her side of the family. So, when I see her face, I am put in mind of you."

"Forgive me for going so far away from you. It was needful for us three to be a family where my wife's 'big house upbringing' as you would say, wouldn't keep me from being able to make my way in the world and provide for them."

"Here I have the opportunity to join the militia. Colonel Spencer is recommending me. It is more pay than I could make in a month, if I had stayed. And if there is war, as many speculate, I will fight. Pray that God keeps me, so I may return to my family and to you."

When she finished reading the letter, she folded it, returned it to the packet and retied the ribbon holding them. She didn't have the heart to read another. She knew the reason her father was never able to return.

Uncle Percy put words to what she was thinking. "And he ne'er come back to us. It's as if the war took him from us, as surely as if he had been kilt in it."

"In a way it did," Lily replied. "After he lost his leg in the war, he didn't go out at all. Though Mother did encourage him to try. He would tell her that it hurt too much."

"Maybe the hurt was in his heart," her grandfather said. "'Tis a blow to any man to not be able to work to keep his family fed and under shelter."

"Yes, I suppose," Lily replied thoughtfully. "It was due to Colonel Spencer that we had a home. He gave father a monthly stipend and my mother kept house for them, and then I went as a kitchen maid when I was old enough."

"It is good that your hands have known work," her

grandfather said, patting her now gloved hand. "Those that are high-born don't always feel pity for the troubles that such as we have, just to keep body and soul together.

"Yes, Grandfather," she said, feeling a bit guilty for not having to work now, due to her uncle's benevolence. Her hands had grown soft. She had felt pride at her ability to contribute to the family income.

Lily had much on her mind on the ride home and stayed quiet. Uncle Nael finally thought to draw her out by commenting on how enjoyable the children seemed to find the picnic by the stream.

Lily nodded, but didn't reply. He tried again to engage her. "Would you be amenable to visiting Widow Hyde and her children again at Doctor Samuel's home tomorrow?" he asked. "Or perhaps we should invite them to dine with us?"

Lily looked up. He finally had her attention. Or so he thought. "I think you should build a vicarage in Hanson's Hollow," she said. "And provide a living so that a vicar can be installed there. And afterward build a school or perhaps the church could double as a school during the week."

Uncle Nael was taken aback. "Is that what you've been thinking on all this time?" he asked.

"Uncle, just think of everything we have seen there. They don't have any education nor preaching. But a vicarage with a small chapel that could double as a school during the week would provide that. My cousins could go to school instead of working the fields."

"I think you have overlooked something," Uncle Nael replied.

"What?" she asked.

"People like those who live there are very transitory. They move frequently. And their parents are more interested in them working for wages than they are taking time away to learn their letters," he said.

Lily scowled. "Luella wants to learn. She told me so when we were by the stream. I intend to bring a children's book for her to start with when I come next."

"You are a kind soul and your cousin a rare girl among those that live there. But they'll likely choose to marry her off soon rather than have her go to school."

"Marry her off, Uncle! How could they? She isn't even as old as I am and I've never given a thought to getting married," she protested.

"I'm glad to hear it," Uncle Nael replied with a smile pulling at the corners of his mouth. "As I have no intention of letting you marry anytime soon. But it is not the way with the poor. If their daughter marries it is one less to keep."

"Uncle! It is not as if she were livestock. She should be taught to read and write."

"She should, I agree. But it is not likely that she will. When you were frolicking at the stream, your Uncle Percy proudly told me of a Joshua who had come calling on Luella. He thinks she may soon be engaged."

"Oh no, Uncle! I will not have it. Luella should go to school, not keep house for some field hand!"

"She may very well like this field hand and be happy to marry him," Uncle Nael countered.

Lily shook her head. "She is too young," she declared. "My father would never allow it. Why would Uncle Percy?"

"Dear Niece," Uncle Nael soothed. "We have only

just met these people. It would be impossible to change everything about their lives overnight. Though I applaud your intentions."

"But the vicarage?" she asked. "Will you agree to build one?"

Uncle Nael laughed. "You have such grand plans for me. But you forget that Lord Hanson is the landowner. He would hardly agree to me establishing a vicarage within the boundaries of his land."

This quieted Lily for a moment. "Would you ask him?" she finally suggested.

"Ask him?" Uncle Nael laughed again. "You have no idea how things work among the upper class. Lord Hanson would be affronted and question my motives. He would not agree and would throw me from his property."

"Perhaps I should ask him," Lily said. "He might be more amenable to female persuasion."

"You will not!" Uncle Nael exclaimed. "You will not use your 'female persuasion' on a grumpy old landowner. I am not even acquainted with the man. And you certainly have not been introduced to him. It would not be proper to approach him."

Lily put the argument aside, but she would not give up. "I will agree to visit Lady Hyde and the children tomorrow if you agree to accompany me back to see my grandparents the day after so I may bring Luella the picture book."

"You are an incorrigible young lady," Uncle Nael scolded. "If I follow your lead, we'll be traipsing all over the countryside every day."

"Well, then two days after to give you a day to rest up, since you are so old and crotchety yourself."

Uncle Nael laughed. "Forgive me, Niece. I am very used to having my own way. You have disrupted my sense of balance."

"Well, I guess I should take myself back to Colonel Spencer's and take up my duties as a kitchen maid," Lily said, feigning offense.

"Very well," Uncle Nael sighed, "in three days time we will return to see your relations so you may bestow your picture book and teach them all to read," Uncle Nael said.

"Uncle! You shouldn't tease so. I mean to help my relatives, if I can. And I mean for you to help me, help them," Lily protested.

"And I shall, if I can, Dear Niece," Uncle Nael replied. "Now let's not argue about the means since our intentions are in unison. Besides, I'm hungry and I can't think when my stomach is talking to me. Let's hurry up the lane so we can ready ourselves and get to the table."

Planning a Tea

But Lily would not let the idea go so easily, and brought it up at every meal until Uncle Nael promised he would try, even though he knew it wasn't likely that he would have an occasion to be in Lord Hanson's company.

He mentioned it to Dr. Samuels when they went for their visit and Lily was pleased to hear him say that he was acquainted with the Hansons and that he would be pleased to make an introduction.

Uncle Nael was chagrined. He was sure that he would never run in the same circles as Lord Hanson and thus never have an opportunity to keep his promise to Lily. But now that she knew an introduction was possible, she would never let the idea go.

"I think it is a marvelous idea," Widow Hyde said, when Lily explained the plan to her. "I don't have any money of my own to commit, but I'm sure I can prevail upon my brother to contribute something."

"Oh yes," her daughter Hannah added. "We should take up a subscription and raise money for the project."

Lily loved Hannah for her enthusiasm. "Thank you. I was beginning to become discouraged. Uncle seemed to think it was impossible."

Widow Hyde came over and sat next to her. "What men think is impossible, Dear, just means it needs a woman to do it. There is a Lady Hanson isn't there?"

Lily had not thought of that! How nice it was to have a woman to confide in again like she did with her mother. "Uncle seems to think I'm trying to upend the whole order of things, but my parents said that the differences between the classes amounted to no less than a lack of education and religious training. I'm sure my Father would want me to help my relations if I'm able. And I can't seem to let the idea go."

"Then we shall make it happen, my Dear," Widow Hyde said encouragingly. "It would not be proper for Hannah or I to hold a Tea for our neighbors since we are still in mourning and newly arrived in the neighborhood, but you could do it and invite the women in the area. If you want to get something done, you start with the women."

"Oh!" Lily exclaimed. "Me? Give a Tea? I wouldn't know where to begin!"

"We could certainly help her, couldn't we Mother?" exclaimed Hannah.

"Of course," Widow Hyde said reassuring Lily. "We can help behind the scenes, but you must be the hostess."

"And you will be there?" Lily asked. "My parents never entertained company, although when I was kitchen maid for the Spencers, Mrs. Spencer often held Teas. But I never went above stairs, I only know what foods to serve."

"Well, that is a start," Widow Hyde said, laughing. "Hannah and I can guide you for the rest. Our circumstances with Mr. Hyde were not as exalted as my brother, the illustrious Dr. Samuels, but we held Teas. It is amazing what a room full of women can accomplish, and it will only take a well-placed word before Lady Hanson takes up the idea as her own."

"Truly?" Lily breathed, her eyes wide with wonder. "I thought I should have to convince the whole world of the merit of the idea."

"Well, it is better to approach the subject

indirectly," Widow Hyde advised. "Let me handle that end and Hannah can help you with the serving. And I think you should invite Luella."

"Invite Luella?" Lily asked thoughtfully. "I'm afraid she'd feel more awkward than I."

"She may feel more comfortable helping in the kitchen, Mother," Hannah suggested.

Her mother shook her head, "No, she must be seen so that the women can be impressed with someone that could be helped."

"I will not put my cousin on display to be gawked at," Lily protested.

"No one will gawk at her, I promise," Lady Hyde assured Lily. "I will be subtle. Now the first thing to do is to set a date and prepare the guest list."

Lily marveled as Lady Hyde took charge of the Tea. She told Luella about it on her next visit. "Are you pleased?" Lily asked as Luella grew quiet.

Luella shook her head and smoothed her dress out. "I don't think so, Miss Lily," she said. "Mam would ne'er agree to let me go to the big house. She counts on me to watch the little 'uns and I have my work here. And then there be Joshua."

"Joshua?" Lily asked. "You want to be married to Joshua?"

"Well, Pap thinks I oughta' and I'm sorta' promised. He and Pap made the bargain night afore last."

"But you want to go to school," Lily protested. "You told me you want to learn!"

"I'm too old for learnen, Mam says. But I do dearly love the picture book you brung me," Luella said, caressing the cover. "Read it to me one more time. I want to remember every word so I can show my own young uns when they start coming."

Lily frowned, but relented when she saw the hurt look on Luella's face. She smiled for her benefit. "No, this time you read it to me," Lily commanded. "You know the words well enough and you need to practice."

Luella smiled shyly. She leaned her head on Lily's shoulder. "I never met a kinder soul than ya', Cousin," she replied as she opened the book and began to read.

Lily kissed the top of her cousin's head and wrapped her arms around her. She thought about Lady Hydes's advice. She would have to be subtle and indirect when she spoke to her aunt about allowing Luella to come up to the house to stay with her for the Tea. She needed to find out what would motivate Aunt Millie.

"Money!" Uncle Nael told her when she asked on the ride home. "It's obvious."

"Money?" Lily asked. "What makes you think so?"

"They are poor with too many mouths to feed. It's likely that the arrangement of her marriage to Joshua comes with a small exchange of money or goods for her family. To compensate for the loss of a strong worker."

Lily was horrified. She had never heard of anything so inhumane. To sell a girl as if she were a prize pony! "My father would never allow such a thing to happen to me."

Uncle Nael laughed, "I shall take that under advisement and not look for a cow to trade you for."

"Uncle!"

Uncle Nael laughed again. "That would never do. I pity the man who tried to take you in hand and tame you."

"That is unfair, Uncle," Lily protested. "Why is it that a woman may not speak her mind, or make decisions for herself, especially when it comes to the matters of the heart?"

"You sound just like your mother," Uncle Nael said. "And we know she chose for herself against our parents' wishes."

"But Luella certainly won't," Lily replied. "So, we must find another way to free her from this marriage."

"Have you asked her if she wants to marry him?" Uncle Nael asked her.

"She is so young, Uncle," Lily protested. "She shouldn't have to make a decision about marrying anyone."

"For many women it is the highest ambition of their lives to marry well," Uncle Nael said. "And for the poor it becomes a necessity. I hope when your time comes you will take my advice on the matter."

"Uncle Nael, I have no thoughts of marriage. I have no intention of letting you get rid of me that easily."

Uncle Nael laughed. "I certainly would miss you, but I am determined to do what I can for you. I have my responsibilities, and should I keep letting you out in public, soon young men will start lining up seeking your hand."

"Will they?" Lily asked, amused. "Is that why you continue to press me to have a party?"

"Well, most young ladies have a debut to be introduced to society. You have not had anything of the kind, and I feel like I should be introducing you to the right sort of people."

"Are Lady Hyde and Hannah the right sort of

people?" Lily asked, teasing.

Uncle Nael's cheeks colored. "Mrs. Hyde and her children are enjoyable to keep company with. Though the boys are quite rambunctious."

"The boys need a steady hand," Lily agreed. "I think they are too old for nannies. They should be starting on an education of their own. I'm surprised Dr. Samuels never thought of it."

"They are still adjusting to their life here, but I think you may be right. I'll mention it to Dr. Samuel's the next time we visit."

"No need to wait so long. *Widow* Hyde and Hannah are coming to see me to plan the Tea."

Uncle Nael flushed again. Lily took note that every mention of Hannah's mother put color in her Uncle's cheeks.

"What pretense have you thought of to get Luella here for the Tea?" Widow Hyde asked when they came to help Lily with her plans.

"None yet, though Uncle said my Aunt Millie would be motivated by money, so I thought I could offer to pay her to come and help serve," Lily answered. "But I don't want to lord it over my relations when I would much rather have her as my guest. Do you think it would seem as if I'm looking down on them if I offered such a thing?"

Widow Hyde was thoughtful. "It may. From your description, your aunt already seems to think that the wealthy do nothing but look down their noses at people like them."

"And she will think I am just like my grandparents who wouldn't even speak to Grandfather William when

60

he came to ask after my Father," Lily said, dejectedly. "If I could only think of another way to get her here simply as a friend."

Unfortunately for Lily, what presented itself came in the form of a tumble off of Bronnie when she tripped on a root. It was the first time Uncle Nael had let Lily ride out alone and when she rose to stand, she felt an unbearable pain in her ankle. She cried out and sank down again.

She sat there for a moment with tears staining her face. She couldn't think what to do. She had only wandered as far as her parents' trysting tree and was still in sight of the house. If only Uncle Nael should look out he would see Bronnie standing there grazing. But then she remembered that he had gone to Dr. Samuel's. She knew it would be an hour or two before he came back again.

Lily tried again to stand without bearing down on the afflicted ankle. She used Bronnie to steady herself and thought if she kept ahold of the saddle and leaned into Bronnie she could hop on her one good foot.

"What's this, Miss?" she heard, interrupting her attempts to move forward. It was Mr. Maginty, the trainer who had given her riding lessons. He was accompanied by someone Lily could only guess was his son as they were so alike in features.

"The horse stumbled," she stammered. "And I fell. My ankle is hurt. I can't walk."

"Ah, well then. Dathan here will set you to rights. Give me your reins, Son," Mr. Maginty directed. "I'll take your horse while you lead hers."

Dathan nodded to Lily and then lifted her back on

her horse. Lily's cheeks burned. It felt like the young man was taking liberties, though she couldn't think of another way for her to regain her seat. He was a fearfully handsome young man, however. But the painful jerking caused by the horse's movements quickly sent any other thought from her mind as he guided Bronnie back to the house.

"I'm afeared you'll not be riding any too soon," Dathan said as he lifted her from the horse and carried her inside and placed her on a sofa. At the sight of her, Cecelia became frantic and summoned James to ride to Dr. Samuel's house to fetch him and Master.

Mr. Maginty had to tell her to remove the riding boot before her foot swelled. The operation was extremely painful to Lily, but Cecelia succeeded in getting the boot off.

"Thank you for your kindness," Lily said to Dathan and his father as she tried to smile through the pain."

"Twas nothing," the young man said, suddenly seeming shy. "We'll see to the horse. Make sure she is put up proper. And perhaps I could call tomorrow to see how you be?"

Lily nodded. At that moment she didn't care. He was a kind young man, but her foot was in too much pain to think of anything else.

It seemed ages before Dr. Samuels came with her Uncle. Cecelia tried cold compresses, but if anything touched her ankle she cried out in pain. It started to swell and turn all sorts of colors. Mr. Maginity's warning about getting the boot off had not come too soon.

Uncle Nael and Dr. Samuels came in together and Uncle Nael rushed to Lily's side. "Dear Girl!" he cried.

"How bad is it?"

"I've never felt such pain, Uncle." Lily replied. "It looks horrendous, and feels worse."

"No wonder," Dr. Samuel's said after examining the ankle and lower leg. "It is clearly broken. It will have to be set right and then you must stay off of it."

"Off of my foot?" Lily grimaced as he felt her ankle and foot. "For how long?"

"Several weeks," he instructed. "It has been my experience that these types of breaks could take up to two months to heal."

"Two months!" Lily protested. "But the Tea!"

"The Tea will wait," Uncle Nael assured her. "I will send word immediately to Lady Hyde and Hannah. They can call when you are up to company."

Lily nodded. "The good news is," Dr. Samuels continued, "that once the bone is set right the pain should lessen. Cecelia, bring some strong drink for Miss Lily," he instructed.

When the bottle was brought, Dr. Samuel's added a few drops to the glass before pouring in the dark brown liquid. Lily didn't care what it was as long as it lessened the pain, but she grimaced at the taste.

"Take a little more, Dear," Uncle Nael instructed. "I know you are not much used to alcohol, so you shouldn't need too much."

Lily nodded and took another sip. She coughed, but was pleased that it seemed to be making her feel drowsy.

"Now this part will hurt," Dr. Samuels said. "There's no help for that. Nael, sit here and hold her. Cecelia, I need you here. It will be fast, Lily, but the movement will cause some momentary increase in pain. Are you ready?"

Lily wasn't sure she was, no matter how drowsy she was beginning to feel, but she nodded, and Dr. Samuels swiftly moved the bone back into place. Lily cried out and the tears began to flow again.

"It's alright, my Dear," Uncle Nael soothed. "I am here." Lily clung to her Uncle, sobbing. It was times like these that she missed her parents most.

As the pain began to subside, from the righting of the bone and the drink and the drops, Lily quieted. She leaned back on the sofa as Dr. Samuels bound the leg to keep the bone in place. "Thank you, Dr. Samuels," she whispered, wiping her eyes.

Dr. Samuels smiled. "Of course. I was not about any business but beating your uncle at cards. As soon as you feel up to it, send word and my sister and Hannah will drive over to visit you."

It was a good week before Lily felt up to a visit, but as soon as her company arrived Lily immediately apologized for having to cancel the Tea they had been preparing for.

"On the contrary," Widow Hyde said. "This is perfect."

"How is this perfect?" Lily asked. "I can't walk. And I'm supposed to keep my foot up. I don't know much about being a lady, but I don't think I should greet my guests reclining on the sofa."

"You can send for Luella," Lady Hyde said. "This is the perfect reason to call for her. She can come and assist you."

Lily's brow furrowed and she tilted her head

thinking hard. "I like the thought of sending for Luella. And I don't think they would prevent her from coming, but why must we have the Tea as scheduled? Why couldn't we postpone it?"

"Think about it. We want Luella here for the Tea. Now you have a pretext for sending for her and since she will be here to help you out, we might as well have the Tea. If you wait until your leg is better, she will have no reason to stay," Lady Hyde said persuasively.

Lily couldn't quite follow the Lady's logic, but she agreed. She certainly could use Luella's help. "I'll ask James to go and fetch her," she said. "And I'll not cancel the Tea just yet, but it's only a month away. I do not feel prepared to entertain at the moment."

Hannah clapped her hands in delight. "Mother will direct everything, don't worry," she told Lily.

The trio was deep in conversation when Uncle Nael returned. He turned aside, not wanting to disturb them, but Lily spotted him and called out for him to come and join them.

"Uncle, may I have leave to send James after Luella? I'd like her to come and help me until my foot is mended."

"Of course, Niece," Uncle Nael replied. "I'll send for him now, but please excuse me as I have no wish to disturb your conversation."

"Nay Uncle, come and sit with us," Lily insisted. "I am tired of talking about Teas, and would like to hear some news."

Uncle Nael smiled. He knew that Lily had no interest in Dr. Samuel's rendition of who was suffering from which ailment. She had a way of trying to throw him

65

and the Widow together. Not that he minded. He gladly took a chair while Cecelia was sent to fetch James.

"Are those flowers from my garden?" he suddenly asked, getting up to inspect the vase that had been placed on the end table. "I don't remember anything like these."

"Oh no, Uncle," Lily replied. "Dathan brought them. The young man who brought me home when I took that spill off of my horse," she explained to Hannah and her mother. "He's promised to ride her until I mend. He says she'll forget her lessons unless she gets ridden regularly."

Uncle Nael looked serious. "Dathan? I'm not keen on you having a caller."

"I would hardly call him a 'caller', Uncle," Lily protested. "Was it wrong of me to agree to let him ride Bronnie?"

Uncle Nael shook his head. "No, he's right about keeping the horse ridden. We don't want her getting lazy while you are mending, but don't encourage him in any other direction."

Lily laughed at her Uncle. "Uncle, please. The thought never crossed my mind. He just came to inquire after my leg and thought the flowers would please me, which they do."

Hannah smothered a giggle. "The thought might not have crossed your mind, but it may have crossed Dathan's," she said.

Lily frowned. "Really? I've never had a young man bring me flowers before. I thought he was just being kind."

"He had better not be getting any ideas," Uncle Nael protested. "I will not have someone like him to call on my niece!"

"What do you mean, Uncle? Someone like him?" Lily asked, the color rising in her face. "He is a perfectly respectable young man and I see no reason why a respectable young man shouldn't bring me flowers or call on me for that matter," Lily replied, truly angry now.

Uncle Nael realized his mistake at once, but he wouldn't back down this time. "If he wants to call on you, he must have my leave and I will refuse to give it. You'll not make the same mistake your mother made!"

"Uncle!" Lily cried, tears springing to her eyes.

Stubbornness and Welcome Company

Nael Mildenhall sat at the dinner table in stony silence and growled at the empty chair at the other end. "Why does she not come down?" he demanded of Cecelia.

"She says her foot is not well enough," Cecelia replied, timidly.

"Balderdash!" he said, banging the table. "She knows I will assist her so that she doesn't have to put any weight on her foot. It isn't good for her to stay abed all day. Besides I hear her thumping around up there. It has been two weeks since she injured herself. It is well mended by now."

"Perhaps it isn't her wounded foot that is bothering her," ventured Cecelia, before she turned on her heel and left the room.

"Such a stubborn girl," he growled. "I am responsible to make sure you make a good match and I will not allow you to wed the son of a horseman," he yelled to no one in particular.

Lily could hear her Uncle's ranting even if she couldn't distinguish the words. It only served to strengthen her resolve. She would not give in, even if she had no real interest in Dathan.

Uncle had no right to insult her father the way he did. She felt she'd never be able to forgive him and was determined to continue to take her meals in her room. It would serve him right to have to eat alone.

Her thoughts were interrupted by a soft rap on the door. "Miss Lily," Cecelia called. "Tis Miss Hannah come to visit."

"Come in Hannah!" Lily called. "I'm so glad to see

you," she said, hobbling over to greet her friend. "I'm in need of company."

"You wouldn't be so in need of company if you would relent and go downstairs," Hannah replied.

"Humph!" Lily said, sounding a lot like her uncle.

"Actually, I have been sent to fetch you down. Mother and Uncle Duncan are down there trying to soothe your uncle's ruffled feathers and I am to convince you to come and speak to him. Will you consider it for my sake?"

Lily laughed. "You are a dear friend, and your mother a saint to take on Uncle Nael. He is so stubborn."

"Yes, and so are you," Hannah said. "Mother and I quarrel, but we could never stay angry for so long. I don't know how you can do it. I would have relented long ago."

"It was a vile thing to say, Hannah. You were there. How could he say such a thing about my father?"

Hannah shrugged. "I don't know why he said it, but in a way it is a compliment to you. My father was the same way. He never thought anyone was good enough for me. There was a young man who wanted to call, but Father forbade it," she sighed.

Lily took her friend's hand. "I am not so silly as to care a whit for Dathan, though he is fiercely handsome."

"Yes, he is!" Hannah giggled.

"But my father was wonderful to me. He was kind and loving. I wouldn't trade him for ten rich men. And neither would my mother," Lily protested.

"I'm sure you will have much to say about who you will marry," Hannah said, smiling. "But men like your uncle and mine feel a tremendous responsibility for us, so my mother says. He only wants the very best for you."

69

"Father and Mother were my whole world," Lily sighed. "I never thought of leaving them for anyone. I wanted to stay in that little cottage where I was loved dearly, forever."

Hannah hugged her friend. "I miss my father too," she whispered. "I wish he was here to advise me."

Lily smiled. "Well, if he's anything like my father, he never wanted you to grow up. Mine wanted me to stay his little girl forever. He didn't want me to leave home."

"Maybe that is what your uncle fears. He always confides to Uncle Duncan that he doesn't know what he'll do when you get married and leave. You've brought such joy to his empty home."

Lily was thoughtful. "Thank you, Friend. I have no intention of marrying anyone anytime soon. I have no other home than this and I have no desire to leave it."

"Then you'll come downstairs? You needn't say anything to your uncle. Just come and be friendly to Mother."

"I will come, but you must help me. It still pains me greatly to use this foot."

"When is Luella coming to help you?" Hannah asked as she helped Lily up on her good leg. "Lean on me."

"Soon, I hope," Lily replied as she hopped on her good leg toward the door while holding onto her friend. "Uncle refused to send for her since I was being so 'difficult' as he put it, but Cecelia was able to get a note to Dathan to fetch her."

Hannah stopped short. "You sent a message by Dathan?" she asked, astonished.

"I could think of no other way," Lily replied

70

nonchalantly. "James would not defy Uncle, but Cecelia just thought she was delivering a note to a friend."

"You're encouraging him!" Hannah cried. "He will think you are serious! It is unfair to use him so, just to get around your uncle."

Lily was thoughtful. "I'm sure you are right. I wasn't thinking about how Dathan would feel. I will have to set him straight."

"And you should do it soon," Hannah declared. "You can not continue to let him think he has a chance when you clearly feel nothing for him."

"You will have to advise me, my friend. I have no experience in these affairs."

Hannah laughed as she helped her friend to the top of the stairs where she could take a hold of the banister, to the great relief of her mother who was beginning to fear their mission to restore peace was in vain.

Doctor Samuels jumped to his feet to help Lily on the stairs. Uncle Nael hesitated, but did not like the thought of Lady Hyde seeing him be discourteous to his niece. He quickly followed and the two men between them brought Lily down into the parlor.

"Thank you," Lily said, as she settled into the sofa and Doctor Samuels elevated her injured leg.

"I'm so glad to see you about," Lady Hyde began. "I have been worried for you. And with the Tea scheduled for two weeks from now!"

Lily was tired of thinking about the Tea. She would not make a good hostess, she decided, as she really had no interest in such things, but as Hannah's mother often said, they were a means to an end.

However, since Lily had broken her ankle, she hadn't thought much about the vicarage and school she had proposed. Her interests had been much more self-serving lately and the thought gave her a twinge of guilt.

"Don't worry about anything," she heard Hannah say. "Mother has everything well in hand. She has a knack for such things."

"I certainly wish she was hosting instead of I," Lily countered.

"Oh my Dear," Lady Hyde soothed. "I enjoy socializing. As does Hannah, but it need not be the same for everyone. You only need to be yourself and discuss how having a vicarage and a school would benefit the area. It is your passion the ladies need to hear."

Lily smiled. She was thankful that Lady Hyde reminded her of it. She had been selfishly sulking these past two weeks. Feeling sorry for herself for the pain her ankle caused her, and feeling that she was justified in her anger toward her uncle. She must try to do better.

It was at this very inopportune moment that Cecelia came in and announced Luella's arrival, escorted by Dathan.

"What is this?" Uncle Nael seethed, standing up and heading toward the entryway to intercept the young man.

"Luella!" Lily cried, holding out her hands to her cousin as Hannah and Lady Hyde joined in welcoming her. "I'm so glad you've come."

Luella shyly approached the group and settled herself on the ottoman near her cousin.

"I'm glad you sent yar young man for me," Luella

said softly. "It was welcome news to Grandfather that it was only your injury that kept you from us. And Pap gladly gave me leave to come and help, to repay you for all your kindnesses."

Lily blushed at Luella's comment about Dathan being her young man. But as she caught his eye, she saw that he thought the same and she blushed again. It wouldn't do to embarrass him in front of this crowd. She must have a private talk with him very soon.

But if her uncle had anything to do with it, she wouldn't get the chance. Uncle Nael was very roughly escorting Dathan to the door and she could tell from his tone that his words were unkind. She felt her temper rising again.

Lady Hyde noticed Lily's expression and shot her an admonishing look. For their sakes, Lily would not make a scene, but she had some choice words for her uncle as soon as she had the chance to say them.

Luella seemed oblivious to everything, but gently chided Lily. "Why did you not call for me sooner? I would have gladly come to ya."

Lily couldn't help but smile at her sweet-tempered cousin. "I'm glad you are here. Cecelia does her best, but a servant is nothing to a cousin."

Luella beamed at Lily's kind words. "I'm sorry Miss," she said, addressing Hannah. "I can't rightly remember your name. I was all jumbled up when I come in with such a grand house and you all so kind to greet me as you done. My head lost itself and aught that was in it must have spilt out."

Hannah and her mother laughed at Luella's declaration, so much so that she thought they might be

73

poking fun at her. But Lady Hyde quickly reassured her. "Oh, you are as sweet and precious as Lily has said you would be."

Hannah took her hand. "We weren't making fun, truly," she said. "We have been so looking forward to meeting you. And now that you are here, I'm sure we'll be good friends."

Luella smiled shyly "Friends. I'd like that. I ain't had no special friend afore, 'cepting Lily."

"How are your grandparents? Our grandparents, I mean," smiled Lily. "Is the family well?"

"Oh, yes," Luella replied. "'Well, 'cepting Maggie has a cold. Mama says she'll get over it fine. Maggie is stout, but she's afeared for Hazel Grace. She's been doing poorly and Mama doesn't want her to catch nothin'."

"The baby isn't well?" Lily asked, slightly alarmed. "Has the doctor been?"

"Doctor?" Luella questioned. "There ain't no doctor in the Hollow. There's a woman that knows something of roots and such. But Mama's tried the politices and Hazel Grace ain't naught better."

"Doctor Samuels, you must go at once to see to the baby," Lily demanded. "Uncle will see to the bill."

Dr. Samuels, who had been sitting quietly listening to the ladies chatter, hesitated. "Shouldn't I ask leave of your uncle before you guarantee his purse?" he asked. Lily's look told him otherwise and he moved toward the door, explaining to his friend that he had a call as Uncle Nael reentered the room.

Uncle Nael dropped into his chair near the fire. The ladies decided that he looked in no mood to be disturbed, so Lady Hyde proposed they go for a ride. "You have not been out of doors, my dear," she said to Lily. "You look pale."

"How am I to mount the carriage?" Lily asked.

"Luella and I will help," Hannah offered. "And the driver can lift you into the box."

"A day out does sound nice," Lily said. "Let's try it. Will I need a wrap?"

"It is wiser to bring it and not need it than to go without it," Lady Hyde advised.

Lily smiled. She missed having a mother to give her advice. She rang the bell and sent Cecelia for her wrap when she appeared.

"My, isn't that something," Luella exclaimed. "You just tinkle that bell there and someone comes to do your bidding?" she asked. "Usually I'm the one that gets hollered fer, and I have to do the bidding."

"Well, here you are a guest," Lily replied. "Though I certainly will need your help. Cecelia and the others are paid to do our bidding."

"I think I might like getting waited on for a change," Luella said, smiling. "But take care that you don't spoil me too much. I'm much counted on at home."

Lily found the ride around the park quite invigorating. Lady Hyde was right. She had spent too long indoors. Now with Luella's help she could spend time in Uncle's garden as well.

The news from Dr. Samuels about Hazel Grace was a bit concerning, however. He was unsure as to the cause of the illness, but said the baby wasn't breathing as well as he would have liked and had a slight fever. He planned to go again the next day.

After their company had left, Luella helped Lily

back to her room and she showed Luella the next room where a bed was set up for her so she could hear if Lily called. They had their supper alone.

Lily's excuse to her Uncle Nael was that Luella wasn't used to being waited on, but he only growled in answer, so she promised that they would both be down for breakfast.

When night fell, Luella helped Lily into her nightgown before changing into her own and taking the candle into the next room.

Lily snuggled under the covers and was soon very drowsy, but she was interrupted by a call from her cousin.

"Lily?" came Luella's quiet voice.

"Yes, Luella? What's the matter?" Lily called, rousing herself.

Luella came softly in and sat on the edge of Lily's bed. She fumbled with her hands and looked like she meant to say something.

"Luella? What is wrong?" Lily asked, growing concerned. "Is there something amiss with your bedroom?"

"Well, it be like this," Luella began. "You see..... The room is so big. I've never been alone before. I always have some of the young'uns sleeping with me. Would you mind much if I bedded down on the floor in here?"

"You'll do no such thing!" Lily cried. Luella's face fell, but she nodded and moved to go back to her room. "You'll come and share the bed with me. It is plenty big enough," she smiled. "I always wondered what it would be like to have a sister."

Luella smiled and quickly went to the other side of the bed and crawled in. "I very well know what it's like to have a sister, and Maggie kicks."

"Well, hopefully I don't kick," Lily said, laughing. "But you are here to tend to me, so it might be the same."

Luella laughed as well, but shook her head. "No, Lily. A sister you can laugh with and talk to, that's different than one you have to tend to."

"I'm glad you are here, Luella."

The next morning, Lily kept her promise and she came down to breakfast with Luella's help. Luella didn't seem to know what to do with herself once she had Lily settled into a chair.

"Oh, let me help!" she exclaimed when she saw Matilda coming with the serving tray. She had it out of Matilda's hands before the young lady knew what to think.

Uncle Nael smiled at the sweet gesture. "Luella, you are a guest," he chided. "You must allow Matilda to do her job, lest she thinks we brought you here to replace her."

"Oh!" Luella exclaimed. "I hadn't thought of it so." She promptly took a seat next to Lily. She waited pensively while Matilda poured her tea and then stared wide-eyed at the platters of food that were brought in. "But there ain't naught but the three of us. Is company expected?" she whispered to Lily.

Lily smothered a laugh. "No, dear Cousin, Uncle Nael just happens to have a hearty appetite," she said, deflecting attention to her uncle, who couldn't hide the fact that he was delighted to not be alone at table today.

"Dr. Samuels has promised to visit Hazel Grace again today," Uncle Nael said. "I hope he finds her much improved."

"As do I, Sir," Luella replied. "She's so dear to me, I hate to see her ailin' so. And it's so kind of you to send the doctor to her. Mam don't have much use for doctors, but I know she'd welcome the help for poor little Hazel Grace. It'd break her heart to lose her and she was that worried over her."

"Try your sausages, Luella," Lily prodded. "They're very tasty."

"It seems a might lavish," Luella replied. "I never et sausages afore. I'd be content with a bowl of hot porridge."

"If you want porridge, the cook will make you some," Uncle Nael said motioning to Matilda.

"Oh no, Sir! Pray you don't go to no trouble," Luella said with alarm. "I will gladly eat what's here." Matilda stopped and returned to her post. "But if it isn't too much trouble," she shyly added, "perhaps she could make porridge tomorrow?"

Uncle Nael laughed. "Porridge it is then. Matilda you'll inform the cook that we would like porridge for breakfast tomorrow," he directed.

"With whatever berry is in season," Lily added. "And cold cream."

Luella smiled. "That sounds wonderful, Cousin! How do ya think of such things?"

"I have lived in the house of Mildenhall for too long," Lily sighed. "I have forgotten my own humble beginnings. Though they weren't quite as humble as yours, Luella."

"So you admit that wealth and privilege have their advantages do you, Niece?" Uncle Nael said.

"Wealth and privilege should be given to those

who know how to benefit those beneath them in circumstances," Lily replied. "Since I am now the only Mildenhall heir I am determined to help those that I can."

"Suppose I were to marry?" Uncle Nael said to Lily's amazement. If my wife were to bear me a child you would not be first in line."

"Uncle!" Lily cried happily. "Do you mean it? Do you mean to marry? To whom?"

Uncle Nael shook his head. Lily was so contrary. The thought of the Mildenhall estate passing to another heir bothered her not at all. "No, I don't mean to marry at this point in my life. However, the thought had crossed my mind. If someone suitable were to present herself."

Lily thought she could divine the direction her Uncle's affections were turning, but she thought better of saying anything. "I would not mind it for the world. This house is too big for just you and I. And a baby to dote on. How lovely the thought is."

"You wouldn't wish for babies of yar own?" Luella asked.

"Oh no!" Lily declared. "Not for a good long while yet. But having a baby around the house might soften me up for one."

"But, yar young man?" Luella added. "You would leave him waiting all that time for ya?"

Lily looked sheepishly at her uncle. "He isn't rightly my young man." she started to say. She had meant to confess her lack of affection for Dathan to her uncle when they were interrupted by Cecelia announcing the arrival of Doctor Samuels.

The look on his face stopped all thought of anything else and caused Luella to cry out. "Hazel Grace!"

she exclaimed, leaping from her seat and running to him. "What has happened?"

Hazel Grace was gravely ill, Doctor Samuels reported. He was very concerned and he had brought the child and the mother with him. It was too far for him to continue caring for her in Hanson's Hollow and since he was there at Lily's direction he had brought them here to be cared for.

Luella flew out to bring her mother and sister inside, while Lily was left with Uncle Nael. "I didn't know he would do that," she whispered. "Is it alright, Uncle?"

Uncle Nael just shook his head. "There's no help for it now."

"I never thought about how difficult it is for the very poor to get doctoring. When Mother and Father fell ill, Colonel Spencer sent the doctor," Lily said. "I thought I could do the same for my relations. Even though the doctor could not save my parents ," she added sadly. "He whisked me away and I wasn't even with them. I never said goodbye."

"Next you will want me to build an infirmary in Hanson's Hollow," Uncle Nael said, shaking his head, but when he saw the sad look on Lily's face, he added, "It will be alright, Niece."

He pushed back from the table. "I better instruct Cecelia to get them settled in a room."

Lily was suddenly left at the table without anyone to help her. She wondered how she was to return to her room without Luella and as it was a pleasant day outside, she was hoping to spend some time in the garden. Her gaze drifted out the window and she caught sight of Dathan exercising Bronnie.

Thinking to get a better view, Lily used her good leg to push her chair away from the table. It took some effort to pull herself to standing without using her injured leg, but once she was there she was able to use the table to hop close enough to reach the sideboard and peer out the window. Dathan certainly was a fiercely handsome young man, she thought.

"How did you get there?" Doctor Samuels asked, as he reentered the room.

Lily blushed at being caught spying on Dathan, but Doctor Samuels didn't notice as he slumped into a chair at the table. "Are you that worried about Hazel Grace?" she asked with sudden concern.

"Yes," he said. "But I had another motive for bringing her here. The winter wheat is being cut down in the Hollow and the air filled with dust. I thought if I could get the baby into a place where the air was clear, she might begin to mend."

"Do you think it will be so?" Lily asked earnestly.

"Some children's lungs do not develop properly," Dr. Samuels said. "Especially if they are born before their time, as your aunt has told me was the case with Hazel Grace, the parents of those children have to take care not to have them around things that kick up a lot of small particles that they could breathe in. If she improves just by bringing her here, then I think I may be right."

"What does that mean?" Lily asked. "Will they have to move away from the Hollow?"

"I can't imagine they would have the means to do so," Doctor Samuels replied. "But if I know you, you will come up with a plan," he smiled at Lily. "But you never told me how you got to the window. I hope you aren't walking on your injured leg."

"Oh no," she replied. "But I would be embarrassed to return to the table the same way. Perhaps you could come help me?"

Doctor Samuels laughed. "Of course," he said, rising to come to her rescue. "But I did bring you something that should help. It's a crutch that will support your bad leg. I thought you could practice with it in the house and maybe you'll be able to get outside. My sister tells me you are in need of fresh air."

"Thank you," Lily said as she settled back into her chair. "I do miss going out of doors regularly. I was hoping that Luella would help me, but now I'm afraid she'll be devoted to Hazel Grace until she is well."

"I'm sure your Uncle wouldn't mind accompanying you outside. He enjoys spending time with you."

"What are you trying to say?" Lily asked, smiling at the good doctor's obvious intention.

Doctor Samuels smiled slyly. "I know he upset you by objecting to Dathan, but I hope you understand it's only because he is afraid of losing you."

Lily smiled. "He has nothing to worry about. I have no intention of going anywhere, with anyone, including Dathan."

Doctor Samuels seemed relieved. "You must forgive us old bachelors. We didn't realize how lonely we were until our relations needed to come stay with us. And now that you have come, we can't imagine our lives without you."

Tea Time

For the next week, Lily saw little of Luella as the girl took to nursing her baby sister and 'toting for Mam' who refused to eat at the fancy table with the family and scarcely set foot outside the room. She caused enough trouble for the servants though, as she seemed to enjoy bossing them about.

Cecelia bore it well, but the cook was beside herself with all of Millie's special meal requests to 'keep up her strength' and ingredients for strange mixtures to be placed upon the baby's chest with warm compresses.

Dr. Samuels put up with the politices as he said they caused no harm to the child, though the odors were often so strong that the other inhabitants of the house avoided that wing.

But as Hazel Grace improved away from the wheat dust, Dr. Samuel's felt he was on the right course. He warned the family sternly that they must never allow her to be exposed to any air that was thick with particles that could get into her lungs and clog her breathing.

Lily was so alarmed that she prevailed upon Uncle Nael to provide the family a house near his orchards where they could help tend the apple trees and blueberries, and there would be less dust to bother the baby.

Luella was happy that her family was close enough to visit regularly and after her mother and sister left the big house, she often brought Hazel Grace back with her, to Lily's delight.

Their new house was small, but serviceable and within an easy distance by carriage for Lily's visits. She continued reading the letters from her father to her grandparents.

The letters gave her a melancholy glimpse into her parents' lives. They often included stories about her.

"Lily is learning her letters. Bronwyn teaches her daily after she returns from the Spencers even though she is tired from the work. Our little Idyllily has added her name to this letter in greeting." Lily smiled at the clumsily printed letters at the bottom of the note, spelling 'Lily'.

Another letter noted how tall Lily was growing and how proud he was of Bronwyn's insistence that she learn to sew so she could make Lily's clothes herself. She had found an elderly neighbor who was glad for the company of the pretty young wife and her daughter, who showed her how to mend clothes and then to make them.

Lily remembered the woman, whom she called Miss Margaret, as being very stern. She was not allowed to play at her house, but had to sit quietly while she waited for her mother. She was finally given a needle and thread of her own so she could practice making stitches in a spare piece of cloth.

When the day of the Tea finally arrived, having been postponed twice, Hannah and Luella had Lily settled before any of the other ladies arrived, while Lady Hyde took charge of greeting the guests and welcoming them into the ladies' parlor.

Most of the ladies were older, though some of them brought their daughters to meet Lily. Lady Hyde had talked Lily into wearing her hair up. She said it was the only way for the women to take her seriously. Lily had convinced herself that she was playing a part, modeled after Lady Spencer, as she graciously greeted each visitor.

"Thank you for coming!" she said to each lady and their daughters. When they had all arrived, she had close to 20 guests.

"So you are the mysterious niece of Charles Mildenhall," one particularly beplumed and voluminous lady said to her. "Where have you been hiding? I have not seen you at a single function this last year."

"I have been in mourning," Lily replied, rather stunned at her forwardness. "I have only been out of black these last few months, and only at my Uncle's insistence."

Hannah, who was still dressed in black for her own father, squeezed her friend's hand, while Luella sat shyly nearby. She had stayed to please Lily, but would rather have been in the kitchen. She had no idea how to act among all these grand women.

When everyone was settled and the tea was being served, Lily addressed the group, as Lady Hyde had instructed her. "Thank you all for gracing our home with your presence. You do me a great kindness by attending my very first Tea. Since I am now out of mourning, and am endeavoring to do justice to the name of the great house of Mildenhall, I am pleased to be acquainted with the women of influence in the region."

Most of the women thought the little speech very flattering. Charles Mildenhall had been reclusive since the tragedy of his parents' deaths and though they had all heard that he had taken his orphaned niece as his ward, they had never thought she could be so refined with her common upbringing.

Those with eligible sons were sure to recommend

the young lady to them. And the widowed ladies among them thought Charles Mildenhall's niece must be wanting for a motherly figure.

The women chatted with each other and each in her turn came to talk more at length with Lily. Lily tried to turn each conversation to the plight of the underprivileged who lived at the fringes of society with the help of Hannah and Lady Hyde.

Lady Hyde had said it was best not to directly mention Hanson's Hollow, though now that Luella's family had moved to her Uncle's land, she had more influence over the landowner for the care of the poor among his workers as a model to the other landowners around.

"And who is this lovely young thing," Lady Hanson asked of Luella who was dressed in one of Lily's everyday dresses, which she had declared was the finest she had ever worn.

Luella looked up, startled. She couldn't imagine that the great lady could possibly mean her.

"This is my dear cousin, Luella," Lily said. "She is lately of Hanson's Hollow, but her family has recently moved to a house on my uncle's land."

"Hanson's Hollow?" the great lady asked, astonished. "We only have farm workers that rent there. How is it that such a pretty young thing could be from the Hollow?"

Luella fussed with her hands and searched for something to say.

"She is my cousin on my father's side. He was a farm worker there and his family stayed in the area of late," Lily reported.

"Oh," Mrs. Hanson said knowingly. Everyone knew the disgrace of Bronwyn Mildenhall running off to marry a farm hand.

She appeared as if she would move back to her seat when Lily said, "I have decided that it is my duty to make sure my cousins have the learning they deserve. My uncle plans to build a vicarage and supply a living so that services may be held there. He is looking into the prospect of employing a school teacher as well, to provide the children of the workers with some education."

Mrs. Hanson was shocked. "Charles Mildenhall has such means?" she asked. "His land produces only apples and wimberries. He has very few tenants. It would be a waste of resources to supply a vicarage and school for so few. They can go to town for their preaching and learning."

Now Lily was angry. Of course her relations were closer to town now by virtue of having moved to her uncle's land, but it was still quite a distance for those who had no horses or carriages.

"How far is Hanson's Hollow from town?" she asked Lady Hanson, slyly. Do your workers walk the distance?"

Lady Hanson narrowed her eyes at Lily. Determined not to be bested in front of the women present, she said, "Perhaps a vicarage on the border where our land meets your uncle's would be more suitable?"

Her tone was a bit sarcastic, but Hannah ignored it. "Oh yes," she cried. "What a marvelous idea, Lady Hanson!"

"Such generosity!" Lady Hyde added, wishing to

seize upon the opportunity presented.

The other ladies murmured their approval and many said they would be willing to pledge a sum for the building, though the living for the Vicar and a teacher would have to be agreed upon between the gentlemen.

Lady Hanson nodded to Lily. She had clearly been beaten and would look the fool if she did not agree to it now. "If your uncle is of a mind to do this, then I'm certain Lord Hanson will agree."

Many were the times of late, that Lily had promised her Uncle's purse, but she knew that she couldn't back down now. "Of course. Uncle has his heart set on bettering the state of the poor workers he is responsible for. I'm sure Lord Hanson feels the same."

Luella was delighted. "It is a good thing yar saying," she said softly, smoothing her skirt. "I know I'm too old for schoolin' now, but I sure would love for my brothers and sisters to know their letters better. We only have the one picture book that Lily give us. I been trying to show 'em. Maggie took to it right off, but the boys' heads be stuffed with straw."

The women gasped and then stifled giggles at this unexpected speech, but Lily beamed at her cousin. "Luella, you are the kindest and dearest of us all," she said, squeezing her hand.

Luella didn't mind if the other women thought her foolish as long as Lily praised her and Hannah and her mother smiled approvingly.

So it was settled. The women all pledged their support to build a vicarage with a chapel that could be used as a school during the week. Now all that was left was to let Uncle Nael know. It was decided among the three that this task would be left to Lady Hyde.

Her Young Man

At supper that evening, Lily informed Uncle Nael that she would like to invite Dr. Samuels, Lady Hyde, and Hannah to luncheon the following day. Uncle Nael readily agreed as he was partial to their company and summoned James to take a message to them.

"How was the Tea, Lily? Uncle Nael asked. "I'm very proud of you for undertaking it, even though the idea seemed to overwhelm you."

"It went well, Uncle," she replied. "The women seem to think something should be done about the plight of the workers." Lily had learned well from Lady Hyde the subtlety needed to persuade someone to do as she wished.

"And have they decided on a remedy?" Uncle Nael surmised. "And what will it cost me?"

Lily laughed and blushed. Her Uncle knew her too well. "Well, of course the women will have to get their husbands' consent, but I think they will agree when they hear the merit of the proposition."

"And what is that proposition? And what will it cost me?" Uncle Nael asked again.

"Uncle, I didn't think you were so tightfisted," Lily admonished. You are always so generous with me."

Luella sat bewildered at the exchange and whispered to Lily, "You said your uncle agreed?"

"He will," Lily assured her, whispering back.

"And what are you two conspiring about?" Uncle Nael wanted to know. The girls looked at him but said nothing. "Fine, "Uncle Nael relented, "but I'm sure to find out. There is not much to talk about around here and your Tea has dominated every conversation of late. I will soon learn how much you have pledged on my behalf."

Lily sighed. She had pledged a living for the Vicar on her Uncle's behalf, or at least half of one. And if either he or Lord Hanson balked at the idea it wouldn't be realized at all. Her only hope was that the wives could influence their husbands to fulfill the commitments they had made for them.

Lily confided her worries to Lady Hyde and Hannah when they came the next day. But Lady Hyde assured her that she had the situation well in hand.

After complimenting the size of the luncheon and the delicacies the cook had created for them, Lady Hyde mentioned that it shouldn't be surprising, due to the fact that the generosity of Charles Mildenhall was well known and spoken of often.

Lily saw her Uncle Nael smile with pride. He didn't seem to mind when it was Lady Hyde who was using her feminine wiles to get her way, especially when he was the recipient. Lily knew that the fish was hooked and that Lady Hyde would deftly land him.

"And what an enterprise you have all pledged yourselves to," she added. "Such a worthy cause, to better the lives of the workers you are responsible for. How many workers do you have now?" she asked.

"I don't know the number precisely," Uncle Nael responded. "Not so many as Lord Hanson. Perhaps 20 during the harvests. Was the good Lady amenable to your suggestion that they build a vicarage and school in the Hollow?"

"Oh, Lady Hanson had a much better idea," Lady Hyde replied. "She feels the building should be placed on the border between your two lands to benefit your workers as well as theirs."

Uncle Nael was thinking fast. So this is what he had been obligated to. "And the Hanson's have pledged to pay for the building?" he asked hopefully.

"Oh Uncle, we could not let the Hanson's take all the credit," Lily interjected. "All of the women have pledged a sum toward the building and with the vicarage and school benefiting your workers as well as theirs, I thought it only right to undertake a pledge on your behalf."

"Of course, you did," Uncle Nael said, sighing. "I should have suspected as much. My purse has been much lighter since you came here, my Dear."

"Should I leave, Uncle?" Lily asked coyly.

"You very well know I could not bear your going, but I'm going to have to better attend to my business to make sure I still have coin in my hand at the end of the day."

The three women smiled while Luella pondered what it all meant. "Do you wish me to go?" she asked. "Lily is getting stronger and I'm sure she can manage without me."

"You will do no such thing!" Lily cried. "I could not bear to be without you and I still need so much help. Tell her Uncle, please!" she pleaded.

Uncle Nael smiled at the dear girl. "You are always welcome, Luella. You make Lily smile and behave herself better. All of you have brightened my table and I hope it will always be so. I'd rather be poor than have no one to share the riches I have with."

The women smiled. Charles Nael Mildenhall could

not say no to the force of all of them.

It was true that Lily was growing stronger. She could bear some weight on her injured ankle and she missed riding. One morning after breakfast, she convinced Luella to help her out to the corral, even though Luella was deathly afraid of horses. She had seen a man stomped by one, she said, but the man was being cruel to the animal, so perhaps that was the reason for the stomping, she thought aloud.

Bronnie was friendly and Lily assured Luella that if she held her hand flat with the carrot she brought for the horse that she would not be bitten. Bronnie nuzzled Lily for more and found the turnip she had hidden in her pocket.

"You are a scamp," Lily scolded, but the horse took no notice and blissfully munched the turnip.

"She certainly is," the pair heard behind them. They turned to see Dathan approaching on his horse. He dismounted and tied the horse to a rail before approaching the women, tipping his hat and smiling.

"It's yar young man," Luella whispered. "He's fearsome handsome."

Lily decided that she had better get this situation cleared up. "He's not my young man," she said loudly enough for Dathan to hear. "And I am ashamed of myself for letting him think so and using him just to get my way with Uncle Nael."

Dathan looked crestfallen. "Your Uncle has forbade me from calling, but I did hope...," his voice trailed off.

"It was because my uncle forbade it that I encouraged you," Lily replied. "I was angry with him. I do not think it beneath me to consider you, as he does, but I have no interest in having anyone as 'my young man' at this moment."

Dathan nodded. "I need to exercise Bronnie, Miss," he said with a coolness in his voice.

Luella squeezed Lily's arm as Dathan strode away, his pride wounded. "Twas a brave thing you did," she said. "It wasn't right to keep him on the line, when you have no intentions in his direction."

Lily sighed. Her intentions. What were they? She had been in mourning for so long, her whole world upended. With her cousin, Luella, and new friend, Hannah, she was beginning to feel the world righting itself again. She had intended to help her father's family and had instead embroiled herself in an unwanted romance.

Lily leaned her head on Luella's shoulder. She felt small in that moment. Small and ignorant, in need of her mother's wisdom and her father's comfort. She hated having to learn to start over without them.

Luella helped Lily back to the house.

"Uncle," she said when they were at the table for the midday meal. "I fear I am so lost without Mother and Father," she said, beginning to cry. "I relied so on their guidance. And now I have only myself to rely on."

"You have me, Niece," Uncle Nael replied gently. "I will never replace them, but I will try to guide you the best I know how."

"And you have me," Luella added. "And all of us, Mam and Pap and Gran and Grandad. And all the young un's adore ya."

Lily laughed through her tears. "I am just a silly

girl after all. And I thought I was getting quite grown up."

"I hope you are not in too great a hurry to grow up," Uncle Nael said. "It seems no time at all since you came here, and now I don't know what I'd do without you."

"Your life was much simpler without me, you must admit, Uncle," Lily replied.

Uncle Nael scoffed. "Yes, simple, and boring. Now, each day brings something new. It keeps me alert, not knowing if the new will be good or bad."

Lily smiled at her Uncle. He tried so hard to be what she needed.

"Lily," Uncle Nael continued. "Would this be a good time to have a small party to introduce you to the neighborhood? You've met the mothers and sisters, but no one else."

Lily heard Luella gasp and gathered that her cousin would be enthusiastic for a party. Lily nodded. "Yes, Uncle. I suppose it is time, but I am saddened by the thought that Hannah and her mother will be unable to attend as they are still in mourning."

Uncle Nael thought for a moment. He was sad at that thought also. "Perhaps next summer we can hold a larger party and include them. We'll keep this one small and intimate and invite just the closest neighbors."

"And dancing?" Luella asked. "I dearly love dancing, though I don't have occasion for it much."

Uncle Nael smiled. "Then for you we will have a bit of dancing. A light supper as well and maybe some tables of cards. Will that suit you, Niece?"

"Yes, Uncle," Lily replied. "But I don't know how I'll dance with this ankle. It still pains me, though it is improving."

"We'll wait until the end of the month then, to see how your ankle is mending. And you needn't dance if you don't desire it."

Fortunately, for Lily her ankle was mending well and by the end of the month the date of the party was determined. Luella was still on hand, although her presence was no longer as necessary as it once was. But Lily enjoyed her company and even though her Aunt and Uncle relied on Luella to care for the younger children, her presence at the 'big house' meant there was one less to provide for at home and anything Luella could save and share with her family she would. Of course, Lily directed many delicacies to be sent over herself, especially for her grandmother who needed soft foods.

Lily was able to visit with her grandparents every week now. Uncle allowed her to take the carriage and she and Luella would spend several hours there, reading the letters from her father, reading books to the younger children and sitting with her grandmother telling her stories. Of course, Grandmother never spoke back, but her grandfather often did. He was so much like her father in many ways that she didn't feel so lonely for her father when she spent time with her grandfather.

Luella had also developed her own interest. Determined to overcome her fear of horses, she had taken to spending time by the corral making friends with Bronnie and Molly. Uncle Nael had given her leave to try riding Molly when Dathan took Bronnie out to exercise her.

Lily was pleased that Luella was becoming more comfortable riding Molly. As soon as she felt brave enough, she planned an outing for herself and Luella to ride over and visit with Hannah and her mother. It was one of the few places that Uncle Nael had given her leave to ride unaccompanied.

On the appointed day, Dathan readied Bronnie and Molly and helped Lily and Luella to mount the mares. Lily noticed that although Dathan barely looked at her, his gaze lingered on Luella sufficiently to make her blush.

"Luella?" Lily asked quietly as they guided the horses toward the road. "What was that?"

Luella blushed again. "He's been teaching me to ride is all."

"Teaching you to ride?" Lily smiled. "Are you sure that is all?"

Luella frowned. "I'm promised. To Joshua. And even though he's fearsome handsome, and that smile could melt butter...," she trailed off.

"You were saying?" Lily asked.

Luella blushed again. "It's just that he gets my head spinning and I forget all about being promised when I'm around him."

"Luella! You are sweet on Dathan!" Lily exclaimed. "And if the look he gave you says anything, he feels the same."

"You have to help me, Cousin!" Luella replied. "Pap and Joshua made an agreement. And if I had been home with them these past months I'd likely be gone and married by now."

"Do you want to marry Joshua?" Lily asked.

"I do. I mean, I did. I don't know. But if Pap says I must marry, then I don't have a choice, do I?" Luella asked.

Lily was thoughtful. "I don't know. Father was in no hurry for me to marry, so we didn't discuss it. But I don't believe he would hold me to a marriage if my heart wasn't in it."

"My heart." Luella said thoughtfully. "My heart wants to help my family. And stay close to them. Joshua plans to move on once we're wed."

"Suppose we talk to your father," Lily offered. "We could perhaps persuade him to break the engagement with Joshua."

"Break the engagement?" Luella gasped. "Suppose Dathan has no intentions at all toward me, and then there would be no Joshua either."

"You don't have to marry anyone, Luella," Lily said. "If you don't want to."

"I'm not so certain Pap and Mam would agree with you. They made it plain that t'was my duty to the family to marry Joshua."

Lily was thoughtful. "Suppose we ask them to give you more time. Then if Dathan has any intentions, he can declare them."

"How? I should be going home soon, as you no longer need me."

"But I do need you, Luella," Lily replied. "You're like a sister to me. Even without my injury, I would have been so lonely without you. I don't want you to move away with Joshua. I would always want you close by."

"Thank you, Cousin," Luella sighed. "I hope I will always be able to live close by. I don't think I could bear going far away, even for a husband and youngun's of my own. I would miss the boys and Maggie and Hazel Grace too much. If you'll go with me, I'll speak to Pap about it."

"You're always welcome to stay with me," Lily assured her. "For as long as you need, if your father is angry with you. He may be angry with me, thinking I influenced you."

"You have influenced me, Lily," Luella said. "I mean that you showed me that I can speak my mind," she added, answering Lily's concerned look. "I concede that I'm not so bold as you, I just never thought I had a right to my own thoughts and feelins afore. Now I see I do, that's all."

Lily was thoughtful. She thought perhaps her grandfather would understand. She wasn't sure about Luella's father, Uncle Percy, but she was positive that Aunt Millie would thoroughly disapprove of Luella having an opinion of her own and she would blame Lily for influencing her.

"Let's talk it over with Hannah and her mother," Lily suggested as they pulled their horses to a stop in front of Dr. Samuel's house. "Second to my mother, she is the best at giving advice."

Lady Hyde thought the solution was obvious. Luella should also be debuted at the party along with Lily. Her parents would surely allow it, since it would mean the possibility of their daughter being introduced to the eligible men of means in the area.

Luella blushed. "Oh no!" she protested. "The Tea was bad enough, being with all those fancy ladies. I be hoping to dance some, but not to be showed off in front of 'em all. I know I shan't be able to speak a word to anyone for fear they'll find me out."

"It would be such a great comfort to me if you were

there, though," Lily said, squeezing her cousin's arm. "Neither Hannah nor her mother will be able to come, as they are still in morning. And I am frightened of the prospect of a party as well, as I have never attended one. Uncle promises that it will be small. Will you promise to come if I make sure that you don't have to speak to anyone?"

"Oh yes!" Hannah exclaimed. "You could say she is from a foreign land and doesn't speak English well."

Luella frowned. "I can't speak foreign. Besides, their mamas and sisters seen me at the Tea. They'll not be forgetting my speechifying."

The ladies laughed and Lily squeezed Luella's arm. "Oh, Cousin, you are a gem!" she exclaimed. "You are such a joy and it would comfort me greatly if you would attend the party with me. You can simply be my companion and need not have any attention focused on yourself that you would not desire. And whether you choose to speak or not, you will still be my sweet Luella."

Luella said she would be pleased to attend the party, but only as Lily's companion. If her mother would consent to it, that is. And there was no guarantee of that. Lily decided that she needed to speak to Aunt Millie on Luella's behalf, even if she thought Lily was being too forward.

Fortunately for Lily, Aunt Millie was not to home when she and Luella arrived. They had a lovely visit with their grandparents before Uncle Percy came in.

"I'm pleased to see ya', dauter!" he exclaimed, giving her a kiss. "And you too, of course, Miss Lily."

"Lily, is fine, Uncle Percy," Lily replied. "Pretend I'm just your niece and not a miss anything."

"Yes'm," he replied. "I see yar getting around on that leg good now. Does that mean I get my Luella back home?"

"Well, that is what we came to talk to you about," Lily said smiling. "Would it inconvenience you if I had Luella stay for a month more?"

Percy frowned and rubbed his chin. "I don't know if that'd sit so good with her Mam. And Joshua's been by. Walked all the way from the Hollow. Just to see Luella, he said. He be thinkin' you'd be wedded by now."

Luella bit her lip. "Pap, I been thinkin'. Supposin' I don't marry Joshua," she stammered.

Percy nodded. "I was afeared you were coolin' on the idea, Luella. But Joshua is a strong worker, he'll provide fer ya right well."

"But Pap, I don't want to leave you and Mam and the young un's," Luella protested. "At season's end, Joshua will leave and I'd be leaving with him. Supposin' I don't ever see none of you all again. I don't think I could bear it."

Percy folded his oldest daughter into his arms. "'Tis true, I been dreadin' the thought of it as well. But what choice be there? Yar nigh past marrying age and it's hard enough for me to keep us all. Joshua be providin' for ya, better'n I can do."

Luella leaned her head on her father's shoulder and looked at Lily, who had uncharacteristically remained silent until then. "Luella, can stay with us, Uncle Percy. If you'd allow it," Lily squeaked, feeling nervous for her cousin.

"No," he said, shaking his head. "We are beholden to your uncle, more than we care to be," Uncle Percy said.

"It's a debt we cain't repay."

"Oh! Uncle Percy!" Lily exclaimed. "There is no debt. It is I who am indebted to Luella for all the help she has given me while I've been unable to get around. She is a great help to me, truly Uncle. And I was hoping she could help me for another month or so, that's all....," she trailed off.

"Joshua be gone by end of harvest," Uncle Percy said to Luella. "And your chances with him."

"If Joshua loves me, he'll wait," Luella said softly, smoothing her skirt. "He'll be comin' agin in the spring."

"And likely be married by then, too," Aunt Millie said, breaking in on the conversation as she entered the room with the other children. "Yar pledged to be wed to him and wed you shall be," she declared.

"Luella!" the children cried at once, surrounding their big sister.

"Are ya' gettin' married soon, Luella?" Maggie asked. "Am I to wear flowers in my hair, like ya said?"

"If ya wear flowers in yar hair and I marry Joshua, he'll take me away and I'll naught see ya' again, Miss Maggie. Wud ya wish it?" Luella asked.

Maggie looked puzzled. "Is it so, Lulu?" she asked.

"I'd naught see ya?" Luella nodded. "Then I'll not wear any flowers!" she said, determined. "Lulu, can't go so far that I'd naught see her no more!"

Percy looked at the sad faces on his young un's. They had always stayed together. He knew how much it had broken his parents' hearts when William went away. "It'll wait until spring," he said.

"Wait?" Millie exclaimed. "You'll ruin her chances for sure!" she said, wagging her finger in her husband's

102

face. "She's 'bout past her prime as it is. Wait 'til spring and she'll of completely lost her bloom!"

"Remember when I wed ya?" Percy asked his wife.

Millie stopped suddenly at the question and gave her husband a quizzical look. "Where ya be going with this line of thinking, old man?"

"Just that you weren't a maid in the bloom of your life when I met ya," he replied. "But you were a sturdy worker with a fair smile. I thought ya'd do right well for me. And ya always have."

"Pshaw," Millie said with a half smile, swatting him on the arm.

"Luella be thinkin' that she'd like to stay the winter here, and I think spring is soon enough for her to be wed," Percy declared. "If Joshua be the man for her, he'll return in the spring."

"Tis that the last word?" Millie asked.

"Aye," Percy replied. "Tis."

"Well, that's that then," Millie said. "But not a day past May Day. I'll not be takin' more chances."

The Storm

The rest of the visit passed more pleasantly with giggles and squeals from the children as Lily and Luella played games with them out of doors and then a quiet sit by the fire as Lily read one of her father's letters.

Lily teared up as she read her father's words written in her mother's hand telling of the loss of his leg and the resulting employment for his wife due to the good will of the Spencers, and how humbling that was for her.

"But she does it with a good will and cheery disposition," she read. "Even with her pricked fingers from learning to sew for our Lily, she does not complain."

Lily left feeling such pride in her mother. Now having a better idea of the circumstances of her mother's early life, she realized what it took for her to leave that luxury and learn to work as needed. She even taught Lily to sew, at least enough to mend her clothes when it was needed.

"The day's turned frightful warm," Luella noted as her father helped the pair mount their horses. They had declined the use of the carriage, opting to practice at riding and giving the horses some exercise. Dathan had encouraged it and Luella was hoping to please him by improving her skills. Uncle Nael continued to employ him to keep the horses exercised when not in use.

"There's an uncanny stillness in the air too," Lily replied as the horses gained the road. "No breeze at all. It's rather stifling."

"I'm used to being overhot," Luella said. "From field work, but ya might be too warm yarself by the time we git back."

Lily smiled. "I'll be fine, Luella. The kitchen at Colonel Spencer's house could get rather warm too. But here's a bit of a breeze," she said as her bonnet strings fluttered. She pushed the bonnet off her head and let the slight breeze ruffle her hair. "That's better," she sighed.

"The wind is pickin' up now," Luella countered as the horses began to snort. "But they's sniffing something in the wind. Animals know when aught is off in the weather."

"Do you think something's off, Luella?" Lily asked as Bronnie began to dance a little and act agitated.

"Molly don't like it neither," Luella replied. "Maybe we should hurry."

"I think you're right. There's a darkness on the horizon I don't like," Lily replied. They pushed their horses to move faster, although neither seemed to need much encouragement. Bronnie was whinnying and snorting in an unusual way.

"The rain clouds be piling up quick now," Luella said with concern as the clouds began to tower into the sky.

Lily had never seen such clouds before. Then the rumblings and flashes of light from within them began. The girls were truly frightened now.

"There's a raindrop, and another," Lily cried. "We better run for it or we'll get soaked."

The girls let their horses go as the rain started in earnest. The horses picked up speed until they were at an all out gallop.

Neither of the girls had ever ridden that fast before and were in very real danger of being unseated at any moment, but knew they had to risk it if they were to avoid getting caught in the storm.

But it was too late. The clouds let their fullness go and the girls were soon wet through, with their horses shying and hopping with every lightning bolt and thunder crack. But the rain did not relent.

"Flatten yourself to the horse!" they heard Dathan shouting as he came riding up hard beside them. "You'll go faster and you'll keep your seat!"

Both girls tried to do as Dathan commanded, but Luella felt herself slipping as Molly jolted along. "Hold on!" Lily cried as the rain pelted them. She was soaked by the time she reached the barn, but laughed out loud at the state she was in. She stopped mid-laugh when she realized the others hadn't made it under cover.

"Luella!" Lily called out, peering through the thick rain. She briefly caught sight of Luella and Dathan before the rain started blowing sideways. "Oh!" she cried out as lightning flashed and the sky turned an eerie green color.

Lily screamed and dove behind a pile of hay when the next bolt hit a tree very close to where Luella and Dathan last stood. Her dread only deepened as Dathan's horse bolted into the barn, followed by Molly, who was moving faster than usual.

"They'll be dead for certain," she cried out as neither Luella or Dathan followed the horses. She couldn't see through the storm. Lily buried her head in her hands and began to weep. "I've killed my friends!" she wailed.

"Lily!" she heard Uncle Nael calling.

"I'm here, Uncle!" she sobbed back. "But Luella and Dathan! The horses came in without them!"

"Oh, I was so worried for you," Uncle Nael said,

scooping her up from the hay.

"Luella and Dathan!" Lily sobbed. "They must be dead for certain. The storm. There was lightning and thunder and, and... the tree!" she cried.

"No, Niece," Uncle Nael said, shaking his head. "They are here. They are here, Dear One," he said as he pulled the soaking pair into view. "The tree almost got them, it's true, but Dathan grabbed Luella out of the way just as the lightning split it."

Lily sobbed as she hugged her cousin. "I thought I'd lost you too. I couldn't bear it!"

"You'll not be losing me, dear Lily," Luella replied, squeezing her back. "Though I confess that I was that scared. It was Dathan what saved me." Luella smiled her thanks at the young man.

"How many times have I told you to mind the weather," Uncle Nael scolded, attempting to cover his relief that none of them was hurt by being overly gruff.

"Are those tears, Uncle," Lily said, hugging his arm. "Do not stop them, lest I am left to cry alone, I'm that glad that no one is injured from that storm. It came up so fast."

Nael hugged his niece. "You are all I have now, dear Lily. I can't lose you too."

"Nor I you, Uncle," Lily replied, squeezing him back.

The Aftermath

Uncle Nael spent the next morning after the storm surveying the damage. Lily could see the split tree for herself from the dining room window as she sat at breakfast with Luella and Dathan who had to be put up for the night as Uncle Nael would not suffer him to ride home until he was assured the storm had moved on.

Luella and Dathan were too busy looking at each other and chatting about nothing of purpose to notice Lily staring out the window at the still-smoking tree. It put her in mind of the half dead tree down by the stream. She thought it must have been damaged by a storm as well and meant to ask her Uncle Nael about it when he returned from his ride.

Dathan rode out right after breakfast to assuage any worry his parents might have about his long absence in the storm, even though Uncle Nael had dispatched a message with James at first light. When he had learned that Dathan's affections were now directed toward Luella, he had no objection to the young man.

Later, Lily found her Uncle warming himself by the fire in his library. "How bad is it, Uncle?" she asked, seeing his despondent look.

Uncle Nael sighed and stared into the fire. "The apple crop is gone. There is nothing for the workers to pick and they will be forced to move on with no pay from the harvest the apples would have brought. I have never so keenly been aware of their plight as I am now and that is owing to you."

Tears came to Lily's eyes. She thought hard for a moment before she moved to sit next to her uncle and laid her head on his shoulder as she had often done with her father. "I'm sorry, Uncle," she said. "Is there anything to be done? Anything that will help?"

"I am not much inclined to send them away with nothing. Though some are already talking of leaving. I don't know where they would go. The storm was far-reaching. No one in this region was spared."

"I wish we could think of something," Lily replied. "But right now my heart hurts so much my head can't think."

"I'm afraid our plans for a small gathering to introduce you to the area will have to be set aside."

"Don't concern yourself, Uncle," Lily replied. "I'm sure no one will be in much of a mood for a party. I'm certainly not"

"Sir?" Luella said timidly as she came into the room.

"Yes, Luella? What do you need?" Uncle Nael replied.

"Will ya be in need of the carriage, Sir?" she asked.

"Not now," he told her. "Is there some errand you need to carry out? Should I send for James to drive for you?"

"Well, it be this way. I know you sent a message telling my folks that we weathered the storm alright. But I'm wishin' to see them and I expect they be wishin' to see me too. I think it's time I went home."

Lily sprang to her feet and hugged her cousin. She let the tears flow freely. "I would never wish you to go, Luella, but I understand. I've been so selfish, wanting you to stay."

"Oh no, Cousin. I could never think ya selfish. Yar

be so kind." Luella assured her.

"At least let me come with you," Lily insisted. "I would like to see how everyone fared. That storm was so frightful."

"Of course, Cousin," Luella assented.

"I think I should come as well," Uncle Nael said, rising from his chair. "There might be any number of limbs and branches blown down and the horse might struggle with the carriage. I can help James to clear the way."

Once James was summoned and Luella had gathered her belongings, increased in volume by several gifts from Lily, they gathered in the entrance hall while he readied the horses and hitched them to the carriage.

Dathan had returned and he volunteered to ride with the group and help with any hindrances. Luella smiled at the sweet gesture.

It turned out that it took all of the men to move some of the bigger limbs and it took twice as long as normal to reach the house due to the stops and having to ride around downed trees that couldn't be moved.

"Oh!" Lily exclaimed as the apple orchard came into view. It was a mess with the trees stripped of apples and leaves. There was no fruit left to ripen for harvest. "Uncle! What shall we do?"

Uncle Nael nodded. He had seen the damage already and knew that it extended to every tree and every field, including Hanson's which they could all see as they drew close to the boundary marker.

"Is this where the vicarage is meant to be built, Uncle?" Lily asked from the carriage. When he nodded, she sighed. "It was such a dream of mine. How is it to be realized now?"

Luella hugged her cousin. "I hope ya not be quitting that dream, Lily. It would mean so much to the workers and the families. Ya be finding a way. I know."

When they finally reached the house, the girls were startled at how different everything looked. The damage to the house was extensive and Percy was already on the roof patching it with help from Carl and Cecil. Tommy was too little to climb on the roof, but he was put to work picking up the dropped nails and scraps of boards to be used for patching.

When he saw the carriage, Percy climbed down to greet them. "Tis a sad thing," he said. "But the house held out and we're none hurt. And now that I can see with my own eyes that no harm befell my Luella and Miss Lily, I'm much relieved. A message sent by your man there is one thing, but seeing is another. Go on in so the others can wrap you up warm. They'll not be satisfied until they see you've naught been hurt."

The girls went inside as the men stayed to help with the patch work. Dathan climbed up with Percy and the boys as James and Nael set to work setting the porch supports right.

When Lily and Luella reemerged from the house they brought some water and bread for those out of doors. Nael and James kindly declined the bread as they knew the family's stores would soon be low. Lily hugged her cousin when it was time to reenter the carriage for the ride home.

"I'm rightly glad ya be staying dauter," Percy said. "It's been hard bearing your absence and worrying fer ya."

"Yes, Pap. I be that glad. I not be leaving agin for a long while."

Percy nodded and seemed to Lily to look back and smile at Dathan. "There naught be any rush to have you away from us agin."

The ride home was easier as they had already cleared most of the roadway. They came upon Lord Hanson on the way looking over his destroyed crops. "I expect that the vicarage we have pledged ourselves to, will have to wait," he called, with what Lily felt was too smug of a smile.

"Certainly not," Lily cried before she realized what she was doing. "Since the workers will not be harvesting, they can be paid to build the vicarage!"

Lord Hanson scowled. "I see who controls the purse strings here," he huffed.

"My purse strings are not in danger, Lord Hanson," Uncle Nael replied. "Obviously, the loss of this year's crop has dealt us all a blow, but we have made a commitment, you and I. And I for one intend to see it through."

Lily was amazed. She had opened her mouth again and instead of scolding her, her uncle had supported her assertions.

Later, Uncle Nael explained. "Hanson will cheat his workers if he can. Push them to work more for less, all the while crying about how poor he is. If he isn't held to his bargain now, he will find an excuse to never keep it."

Lily beamed at her uncle. She was prouder of him at that moment than at any time since her arrival. "Uncle, how wonderful you are!" she exclaimed.

"Well, the man does get me riled sometimes. He

owns twice the acreage than I do, has double the income and complains that supplying half a living for a vicar and a teacher will put him in the poorhouse. Besides, it is a good idea to put the workers to work on the building instead of sending them away empty-handed."

"Your kindness will be remembered, Uncle. And the workers all the more loyal to you," Lily replied. "I know. The many kindnesses the Spencers showed to my family only served to endear them to us all the more."

"Well, I am not so bad off that I can't draw from my reserves. And whether I like it or not, I have been made so keenly aware of the circumstances of my workers that I can't ignore them in good conscience."

A Harvest Ball

"Mildenhall you are a marvel!" Dr. Samuels exclaimed. "To think of using the farm workers to construct the vicarage and chapel so that they would have work and we wouldn't lose our workers."

"Well, the money had already been pledged," he began, but thought better of it. Sighing, he said, "It was Lily's idea really. Between her, Lady Hyde, Hannah, and Luella I had not much choice in the matter," he said, shaking his head. "Women can be quite persuasive when they take a mind to be."

Dr. Samuels laughed. "Yes, my sister apprised me of the matter including the amount we had pledged. It would do them well to have some knowledge of the accounting before they go dipping their hands in our pockets," he smiled. "But we wouldn't have it any other way, would we, Mildenhall."

"Not a bit," Uncle Nael said, smiling as the group of ladies in question approached, their heads together, talking excitedly about the work being done. How fetching they all looked on this warm day, especially Lady Hyde who had finally given up her mourning clothes and was clad in a pale blue, which matched her eyes.

"Uncle! Dr. Samuels!" Lily called. "Isn't it marvelous! It was such a small seed of an idea in my head and look at what it has grown to. And the workers, Uncle! How kind of you to think of them and provide them employment so they may keep their families."

"Yes, thank you for your many kindnesses," Luella added. "You have been so generous to me and to all my family," she said as she glanced at where her father was helping to lay stone. Even her brothers were employed hauling the stones as they were able.

And Joshua had stayed. He had told Luella that if staying was what it would take for her to agree to wed him then he would stay and find whatever work he could.

The vicarage would need a groundskeeper, Lily hinted to her Uncle and Lord Hanson, as she suggested Joshua for the job. Luella was puzzled by Lily's actions until she told her that as long as she was intent on marrying, it didn't matter to her who the groom was as long as he was kind and gentle to her cousin and she stayed nearby.

The building continued all through the harvest season and into the cold months. And was only interrupted by one significant event and that was the long promised ball. Lily had argued that the neighborhood needed something uplifting and fun to look forward to, but she insisted that everyone was invited to attend, including the workers and their families.

Uncle Nael gave up trying to interject some sense into this new plan of Lily's, especially when Lady Hyde and Hannah chimed in with their excitement and enthusiasm. He couldn't stand against all three and almost wouldn't wish it when he saw the smiles on their faces.

The Mildenhall ballroom had never seen the like of the spectacle. The wealthy landowners dressed in their finery and the lowly workers putting on their Sunday meeting clothes, the best they had. Uncle Percy certainly looked different with his whiskers shaved off and Lily's grandmother beamed as she sat in a chair and watched the dancing.

The workers were shy at first and stood off to the side unsure of their manners. But the table full of cheeses, cakes, and as much fruit as could be had, tempted the more bold among them and they were soon filling their bellies with the delicacies that were scarce commodities in their own homes.

They watched as the orchestra played the stately old music that the more refined in attendance were used to, until Uncle Percy asked to borrow 'a fiddle' as he called it and started playing a 'foot stomper'.

Oh then such merriment that ensued! If anyone's sensibilities were offended they didn't want to own it as their hostess Lily gladly joined in whirling Luella on her arm and even taking a turn with both Joshua and Dathan.

Her younger cousins laughed as they took hands with her and danced a circle dance with Lily as lead. The dance was everything she could have hoped for as each half of her life joined together to make one blissful whole.

"It should always be like this, Uncle," she breathed as she lay her head on his shoulder in that childish way that delighted him. "The well born, should not think they are so far above the low born, and should invite him into their company often. They would both learn a lot from the association."

Uncle Nael smiled. He didn't like to admit his niece may be right, but he had an inkling she was.

Uncle Percy came and clapped him in a strong, sturdy handshake. "We owe so much to you, Sir," Uncle Percy said. "And such a party as we've never had. Look at the sparkle in my mother's eye, if you would. She is that glad of it. To see a day like today."

"Every year, we should host a harvest ball!" Lily

blurted. "Oh, say we will, Uncle."

"Ah, there you go again, pledging my pocketbook," Uncle Nael replied, smiling.

"It is good business, to boot," Uncle Percy added.

"Good business?" Uncle Nael asked. "How so, we've not made a cent this year on the apple crops and have dipped into the stores for this endeavor as well as the vicarage."

"Ah, but the workers work harder and better for them thats treats 'em kindly and is generous as you are. And they are less likely to take a skimmin' for themselves if they feel they are justly rewarded for their efforts. And those that do are pushed out by the workers that are more steadfast."

Uncle Nael nodded. Though the thought of his workers taking 'a skimmin' for themselves' alarmed him somewhat. "It is all due to Lily," he said. "None of this would have been a thought in my head before she came into my life."

"Then she is a blessing to us both," Uncle Percy said. "To have a house and assurance of employment, not to mention the company for my Luella and the rest of us. How our lives have changed since she came."

"Yes," Uncle Nael agreed as Lily went off to dance with her cousins. "Everything is so different now."

"I'll be losing my Luella soon," Uncle Percy added. "Springtime for sure. And those bees buzzing around your Lily seem to have the same intention. I don't know what I can bear it."

"Nor I," said Uncle Nael. "I proposed the ball with the intention of introducing Lily into society, but I don't like the idea of anyone coming to carry her off."

"They'll be lining up now," Uncle Percy said, motioning in the direction of the young men eyeing both their girls and Hannah. "There ain't no help for it. It seems the area has been hard up for pretty young gals 'til they come along."

"They are a force to be reckoned with," Uncle Nael added, glancing at the motherly figure in their midst.

"Do you not dance, Sir?" Uncle Percy asked. "You being a bachelor and all, I think your services on the dance floor should be in demand as there is more than one lady lackin' a partner."

"I think I shall," Uncle Nael replied. "If you'll play another foot stomper. I don't know when I had so much fun."

"Tis agreed then," Uncle Percy nodded. "You twirl that fancy misses around the floor a few times and see if that don't do the trick."

Uncle Nael laughed and headed toward Lady Hyde to ask for a dance while Uncle Percy announced another foot stomper to the delight of everyone.

The festivities lasted well into the night and early the next morning and was much talked of for months to come.

Lily's leg was sore the next day and she wondered aloud if she would always have to favor it. "Dr. Samuels says no, that it will heal. But perhaps I shall become one of those people that can predict the weather by the ache in my bones."

Uncle Nael and Luella laughed. "Come and walk in the garden with me, Niece, to stretch out that ache and warm it in the sun," Uncle Nael suggested, standing up and taking her hand. "You too, Luella. If the number of young men buzzing about the pair of you last night is any indication, you'll have little time for my company."

Lily vehemently shook her head. "No thank you, Uncle. There were none there worth looking at save the two that have their eyes set on my dear cousin here."

Luella blushed. "I don't know whatever I will do," she confessed. "Having two fellers vying for me is a new experience. The moment I think I've settled on one, the other comes along and I think I prefer him. Maybe I'm better off having Mam and Pap pick for me as I can't seem to make up my mind."

Uncle Nael laughed. "Well, I plan on choosing for Lily here, when the time comes, so it will be a good, long while yet."

"Which suits me fine," Lily replied. "I am not yet accustomed to the way some of the rich look down their noses at those of common birth. And those of common birth think me unattainable and do not seek me out. I'm an oddity, to be sure."

The three settled in the garden. Lily commented how grateful she was that the weather had stayed warm so that the work on the vicarage and chapel could continue. They could soon advertise for a vicar, she said, Lord Hanson and her Uncle having agreed on the living they would provide.

When that topic had been thoroughly canvassed, Lily turned her attention to something that she had wanted to ask. "Uncle, I do believe it is time you told me the story of that tree by the stream," Lily said. "It is too much like the one that was struck by lightning during the storm to be a coincidence. Did something similar happen to it? It must be something that pains you to speak of, as you've never offered to tell me."

Uncle Nael looked thoughtful. "Yes, it is painful. And no, I've never spoken of it."

"Will you tell us now?" Lily asked gently.

Uncle Nael sighed. "I find it difficult to refuse you, my dear. But perhaps it will help me to unburden myself. You see, I feel responsible for what happened."

"Responsible? For a storm?" Lily asked.

"No, not the storm," Uncle Nael replied. "Only for what happened. For my father's death."

"Uncle," Lily said softly, taking his arm. "Surely you have no responsibility for that. You said his mind became muddled after Grandmother's death. Whatever happened I'm sure it is because his judgment was clouded."

"Yes, it certainly had. He was overcome with grief and had broken down and asked for your mother daily. I had written to her, to beg her to come, but hadn't yet posted the letter when the storm came."

"What did Grandfather do? Did he die in the storm?"

Uncle Nael nodded. "I could not prevent him. As the wind grew stronger he ran out into the garden shouting for Mother. I tried to pull him back inside. But we were both drenched with the rain and he slipped out of my grasp and ran toward the stream. That's when the tree was struck. He was too close to it. For a moment I couldn't see anything, it was all brightness with the most frightful noise. When it passed, he was on the ground. I, I couldn't revive him, nor Dr. Samuels when he was called."

"Oh, Uncle!" Lily exclaimed. "I'm so sorry. How

awful for you! Is that why you fear getting caught out in the weather?"

Uncle Nael nodded. "When you were caught in the storm, I was so taken by fright that I could barely force myself to run out to you."

"But you did run out, Uncle," Lily soothed. "And we were all saved."

"Not due to me, but I'm glad of it. If it happened a second time, I would think myself a cursed man indeed."

"Isn't it fine that Lady Hyde and Hannah are out of mourning?" Lily said, changing the subject to something that would bring a smile to her uncle's face.

"I know what you are hinting at, my Dear," Uncle Nael replied, raising his eyebrows. "Not that I mind, really. I've been thinking about how lovely it would be to have a woman around the house. She might help me settle you. If I were to marry, she'd have to take my side."

Lily laughed. "And the boys? Who is to settle them?"

"Humph," Uncle Naeil replied. "There's no settling those boys. Wild beasts they are."

Lily and Luella laughed heartily at this proclamation.

"They are good lads," Luella protested. "They don't have no one to make 'em mind is all, now that their Pap's gone. My Mam keeps my brothers in line, but that tisn't Ms. Hyde's way. She is all kisses and kindness. She doesn't know how to be gruff. And maybe the boys will be better for it."

"Maybe so," Uncle Nael said. "But I'll be thinking twice before taking the boys into the bargain."

The New Vicar

The whole neighborhood as well as Hanson's Hollow was buzzing with the news that a vicar was being sent just in time for a real Christmas service. The young ladies of the area were pleased to hear that he was unmarried and the first week he was in the house, he opened his door to many of their mothers with gifts of foodstuffs with their eligible daughters in tow.

Of course, as one of his patrons, Uncle Nael had the young clergyman as his guest on one of his first evenings in the area. He had invited Dr. Samuels and Lady Hyde as well as Lord and Lady Hanson to round out the party.

Lily was glad that Hannah was to be included in the party as meeting eligible bachelors made her very nervous. She feared she wouldn't know how to act and give the young man the wrong impression by being too friendly as she had done with Dathan.

Lady Hyde advised her to ask him questions about his family and where he came from. She said everyone liked to talk about themselves and a well-put question could fill a quarter of an hour.

Uncle Nael told her she needn't worry as he planned for the men, Lady Hyde and Lady Hanson to sit at table within easy talking distance. She and Hannah would be seated furthest away.

"Still trying to keep the young men away from me, Uncle?" Lily teased. "But Hannah shouldn't be punished as well. Perhaps the vicar shows a preference for her."

"Fine," Uncle Nael replied. "She may sit beside her mother and you may sit opposite, next to Dr. Samuels.

We will carry the conversation so you needn't worry."

"Perhaps he will find my lack of conversation all the more alluring," Lily said. "A man who makes his living by giving sermons may prefer a young woman of few words."

"You love to torment me, Niece," Uncle Nael scolded. "I will decide when you are to wed, and you're not to consider it until I give you leave."

"Yes, Uncle," Lily said, smiling. He knew the only reason she was being so accommodating was that she had no interest. If the young vicar caught her eye, however, she would be more difficult to rein in.

Prior to dinner, the party took a tour of the house. It was a grand estate and it surprised Lily that she hadn't seen the entirety of it until then. There was a hall of fine art work that she had never stumbled upon, a small study that had belonged to her grandmother, and a grand balcony that looked over the gardens. As much time as she had spent in the garden, she had never noticed the feature.

She thought the view spectacular and lingered overlong watching the sun dip toward the horizon over the snowy fields.

"It's beautiful, isn't it?" she heard from behind her. She turned to see the young vicar smiling at her.

She looked past him and noticed that they had inadvertently been left alone, which made her intensely uncomfortable. She blushed, which he took as favorable and his smile broadened.

"Sir, the party has passed within," she stammered.

"It would please me if you would call me Daniel," he said, offering his arm to escort her inside.

She felt compelled to take his arm, but let go as soon as they met the others indoors. "Thank you, Mr. Rivers," she murmured as she moved to her Uncle so that she could take his arm instead. As they descended the stairs, Dr. Samuels escorted Hannah, while Lord Hanson had claimed Lady Hyde. That left the young vicar in the company of Lady Hanson.

Lily smiled to herself as she heard Lady Hanson expound upon all the sermon topics she felt the young vicar should take up within his first months there. He assured her that being new to the clergy he had been advised to stick closely to the prescribed ecclesiastical calendar.

"Of course," she beamed. "I wouldn't recommend anything else, but there is always room for some embellishment on your part."

Vicar Rivers nodded. "I will try my best. Perhaps you'd care to give me some notes each week, to help me improve?"

Lady Hanson was quite flattered by this request and assured the young man that she would be a regular visitor at the vicarage as she had many thoughts on the sins of the common man that needed to be addressed from the pulpit.

This line of conversation continued until they reached the dining room and were seated at table, which relieved Lily since she was able to keep mostly to Lady Hyde and Hannah for her exchanges. She was disconcerted, however, to catch the young vicar staring in her direction all too often.

She was glad when they were able to retire to the women's parlor afterward and let the men do whatever men did in their sitting area.

"He's terribly, presumptuous," Lily whispered to Hannah.

Hannah agreed. "When he wasn't looking your way, he was glancing mine. Thinks because he is handsome and learned that he could get anyone just by smiling at her."

"Puts me in mind of Dathan," Lily replied. "I found his attentions flattering at first, but he seems overconfident as well."

"I think he is less pompous than the vicar," Hannah replied. "He is of the working class and seems well grounded. Do you not think he is a good match for Luella?" She asked.

"I don't know," Lily sighed. "I'm just tired to death of Vicar Rivers. I hope he finds a wife soon, so I'll not have to endure him any longer."

Hannah laughed. "I don't know. Perhaps we should hold our opinion until we see how good he is at sermonizing."

Now it was Lily's turn to laugh. "Oh Friend, there will always be someone wanting to matchmake, thinking we must be in want of husbands."

"I wouldn't mind, you know," Hannah said. "Now that we are out of mourning I'd like to think spring would bring a few callers around. When the time comes, I don't want to find myself without any suitors."

"Oh Hannah!" Lily whispered. "If you want suitors, we may have to send away for them, as there aren't many eligible young men in the region."

"What do you think of our young Vicar?" Lady Hanson interrupted, arranging herself near the young ladies.

"He is very handsome," Hannah offered.

"And has quite a confidence about him," Lily added.

"He is quite in want of a wife," Lady Hanson suggested, eyeing them to see how they reacted.

"Is he?" Lily asked, innocently. "We should throw a Christmas party then and introduce him to the eligible ladies in the area."

"Pish, what a scamp you are," Lady Hanson admonished. "He clearly has an eye for both of you young ladies. Would neither of you have him?"

"Lady Hanson!" Hannah exclaimed. "We've barely become acquainted with him."

"We are anxious to hear his Christmas Day sermon, though, aren't you," Lily asked, hoping to change the direction of the conversation.

The girls were happy that Lady Hanson took the bait and commenced to elucidate all of the advice she had given him, as one who knows the area.

"He can't be expected to know the peculiarities of the region, having just arrived. I suggested that he reserve a treatise against strong drink for the New Year, as the winter months find too many men with no employment and in the pubs. I'm only glad that they will be short on money this year, though that doesn't always stop them from using the last of their funds to the detriment of their families."

"Perhaps the cure is employment then," Lily suggested. "When they have aught to keep their hands busy, they are more often home and out of the pubs."

"We have no winter crops," Lady Hanson replied.

"And we will not need a new building every year as we have this year."

"Then we shall have to think of ways to keep the workers occupied through the winter," Lily replied, smiling. "I'm sure if we put our heads together, we'll think of something."

"You are an ambitious one, aren't you," Lady Hanson replied. "I prefer to be content and let those things work themselves out. Besides, a well-placed sermon should do wonders. Nothing like the fear of hell to put a man on the straight and narrow."

"Do you not fear hell yourself, Lady Hanson?" Lily asked with an innocent expression on her face.

Lady Hyde knew Lily's intent was anything but innocent and decided it was time to intervene, lest she take it too far. "Lady Hanson, there are several of us who have committed to decorating the church for the Christmas service. Do you have anything you could lend to the endeavor?"

"Oh yes!" Lady Hanson replied. "But who is taking charge of the project? I fear no one knows decorating as well as I."

"If you are willing to direct us, we would be glad to have you. We plan to meet the day before so we will have plenty of time to complete it for Christmas Day."

"Well, then it is settled," Lady Hanson replied. "I have just the idea that will make it perfection, and a new box of candles fresh from the candlemaker's shop."

"I'm sure it will be lovely, now that we have you to give us guidance," Lady Hyde smiled.

Decoration Day

Lily was excited. It was finally decoration day and they were to meet that morning at the church. Even though the group would include Lady Hanson, Lily knew it would be a day filled with fun and merriment. Hannah was excited as well, because she knew that several of the young men would be there helping, managing the ladders and hanging things at the ladies' directions.

Lily needed help with the boxes filled with her grandmother's items that they were lending for the enterprise and headed toward Uncle's study to ask where James might be. She stopped short when she heard a murmured conversation coming from within.

She had never listened at the door in her life and wouldn't have now if she hadn't caught the following speech from her uncle.

"You've only just arrived, Sir. I don't think it prudent to settle so readily on one young lady," she heard Uncle Nael say. "Besides, you don't know Lily well. She can be quite contrary when she has a mind to. If she decides against you, there is nothing you can say to sway her."

Lily heard a young man laugh. Was it Vicar Rivers? It must be! There were no other new young men in the area.

"There's a fire about her that I like," she heard the vicar say. "She states her opinion quite openly. I like her frankness. She may be difficult to win over, granted, but I only ask your leave to try."

"Say no, Uncle!" she thought. "Please, say no!" But she heard her uncle give his assent and her heart fell. Lily fled to her room. How could he?

Uncle wouldn't just give her to anyone. She knew that much, but why wasn't he making it more difficult for the vicar to pursue her? It seemed like every other man who showed the slightest bit of interest had obstacles thrown in his way by Uncle Nael. But this one had his permission! How was she to discourage him?

"Well," she thought. "If frankness is what he likes, then let's see how he feels about opinionated bossiness. Uncle often tells me how contrary I can be. I certainly can play that part, taking a page from Lady Hanson's book."

Lily swept down the stairs, lifting her nose so high in the air she almost stumbled. "That will never do," she thought, as she imagined herself tumbling down the steps and landing at her suitor's feet. Vicar Rivers was saying goodbye to her uncle with promises of visiting again if invited.

"You are always welcome at table," Uncle Nael said, shaking his hand in keeping with the current fashionable trend.

"I apologize for interrupting, Uncle," Lily said, acting annoyed. "But I need help with the boxes and wondered where James is off to. I sent for him a quarter of an hour ago."

The young vicar immediately replied, "if James is not around, I would be glad to help," he offered.

"I suppose you'll do," Lily said haughtily. "Are you acquainted with harnessing horses? The carriage needs to be brought up."

She thought she was playing her part well, but was a little discouraged when the young man seemed ready to rush to the stables.

"Nonsense, Niece," Uncle Nael interjected, wondering about Lily's strange attitude. "I've already told Dathan to have the carriage ready at quarter past. He should be bringing it up now."

"Fine," she said. "Then you can carry the boxes." She turned on her heel and whisked out the front door where the boxes had been placed earlier.

When the carriage was brought up, Lily barked harsh orders and set the vicar to rearranging the boxes for a full half an hour until she was satisfied that they were placed just right. But she was disconcerted that the young man only smiled confidently and did just as she asked without frustration.

Uncle Nael smiled to himself. "So that's what you're up to, my dear," he thought. "I think you have met your match in stubbornness. When he gets an idea in his head, he looks to see it through."

"May I accompany you back?" Mr. Rivers asked politely. "I'm sure I can be of some use hanging boughs and such."

Lily couldn't think of a reason not to allow it. "I have promised to go by Doctor Samuels' and pick up Lady Hyde and Hannah. There'll be no room in the box," she finally said.

"I'll be happy to play the part of driver and spare James the trouble," Mr. Reeves replied.

"But your horse...," Lily stammered.

"I'll tie him behind," he replied, moving quickly to secure the horse and position himself so Lily could mount the carriage box.

Lily tried to stay angry, but the day was sunny and the ride pleasant. She was warmly tucked up under a blanket in the box and thought Mr. Rivers might be getting cold up on the driver's seat.

She was disappointed when they arrived at Dr. Samuels' house and it was only Hannah and the boys waiting for them.

"Mother has a cold," Hannah explained. "And Uncle fetched somewhere to tend someone, so the boys must come with us."

The rest of the ride was filled with interjections of "Aidan! Aaron!" from Hannah as they tried seeing how far they could hang outside the carriage box without falling out. Her brothers were full of energy.

Thankfully, when they arrived, Vicar Rivers said he had a special job for the boys to do and took them off of Hannah's hands for a bit.

Lily immediately unburdened her predicament to Hannah and Luella who had arrived earlier. "It was awful," she protested. "I didn't know what to say. I kept trying to be mean, but he didn't seem to notice. He's so arrogant. What shall I do?" Lily asked her friends.

Hannah sighed. She had her hands full with her brothers and really didn't have the patience to worry about Lily's preferences in men. Besides, on the advice of her mother, she was warming to the idea of giving the vicar a chance to show what kind of man he might be, before writing him off based on the one impression they had of him.

"It was thoughtful of him to offer to help, don't you think?" Hannah replied finally.

"Yes, I suppose," Lily reluctantly agreed. "But he seems intent on pursuing me even though I have made it plain that I am not interested. There are other young women in the area he could be introduced to. There was no need to settle on me after one dinner together."

Lily paused as she thought about what she could do, since her friend was so distracted. "Perhaps we should throw that Christmas party we suggested and invite the eligible young ladies for him to meet."

"Perhaps," was all that Hannah replied. "Aidan! Aaron! Stop running! Oh those boys! I thought they could be of some help, but they are intent on running wild."

"Maybe the boys would like to go visit my brothers for the afternoon," Luella offered. "The young uns could show 'em a right good time and if they got into any mischief Mam and Pap are there to set 'em right."

"Do you think it would be alright," Hannah asked, grasping at the opportunity to get her brothers out from under foot.

"Of course," Luella said. "The boys don't have no playmates 'sides each other. They can show yar brothers all the best places to play. They'll have to finish their chores first though."

"Chores?" Hannah asked. "My brothers have nothing like chores to do. Perhaps it would be good for them to help."

"Yes, I think it would," Luella replied. "Come, it's only a short walk to the house. We'll take them over to introduce them. They'll have a grand time together."

Lily frowned as Luella led Hannah and her brothers away. She was hoping to have a good talk with someone and there was no one there to confide in.

"Can I help with anything," Vicar Rivers said, coming up beside her.

Lily shook her head. "But I think Lady Hanson has

some projects you could help with. She is directing this operation."

Vicar Rivers smiled and moved to help Lady Hanson. Lily couldn't understand why the young man seemed so determined after having met her just once.

Luella and Hannah returned shortly, and Lily thought to begin the conversation anew when the looks on their faces told her that something was amiss. "What has happened?" she asked with alarm.

"It's Gran," Luella said with concern. "She's ailing. Pap says to come quick!"

"I'm off to fetch my uncle," Hannah said. "I can take your carriage, of course?"

"Of course," Lily replied. "But you'll need to find a driver. Vicar Rivers brought us here."

"And he'll be happy to take you back again," Vicar Rivers said, approaching them after overhearing their conversation.

Lily didn't have time to argue or cast around for another young man for assistance. "Fine. Hannah, bring your uncle to the house as soon as you find him. Please hurry!"

Lily and Luella ran as fast as they could. "What happened!" Lily cried as they got close enough to shout to her Aunt Millie who was keeping the children occupied out of doors.

"She's had t'nother one of those fits, like afore," Aunt Millie replied sadly. "You'll find her laid out in front of the fire."

"Laid out!" Lily said with alarm, thinking the phrase meant that her grandmother had passed, but she found that a bed had been pulled in front of the fireplace and Grandmother had been laid there to keep her as warm as possible.

"Grandmother," Lily called softly as she and Luella knelt beside the bed. "It's me, Lily. And Luella is here too."

Their grandmother moved her eyes to look at them, and Lily thought she detected the faintest hint of a smile.

"See there," their grandfather said through his tears,"she's that glad to see you. It's time for her departing and she'll be wanting to say goodbye to ya."

"No, Grandfather. We've sent for the doctor. He'll come soon," Lily replied, hoping that Dr. Samuels would be able to do something for her."

He just shook his head, and took the hand of his wife, sanctifying it with his kisses and tears. "You've been the best wife a man could ever have," he said. "And the best Mam and Gran to the young 'uns. I don't know what I ever shall do without ya. I 'spect I be follering soon after."

Lily was a little alarmed. There hadn't been enough time, she thought. She should have visited more often! Tears began to trickle down her face.

"Don't give up," she whispered to no one in particular. "The doctor is coming." But she began to feel that her dear grandmother was beyond the doctor's help as she closed her eyes and her breathing slowed.

It would be a long vigil. After several hours the doctor came and went, assuring them that this stroke was much worse than the last and that she wouldn't recover from it. There was nothing to be done but make her comfortable.

Vicar Rivers stayed and prayed, offering comfort to the family, but eventually it grew too late and he left as well, taking Hannah and her brothers back home and leaving the carriage at Uncle Nael's, having appraised him of the situation.

It was only this small band of family who was there to witness her passing in the wee hours of Christmas morning. The woman opened her eyes briefly and lifted one hand toward the corner of the room, seeming to see something the others did not.

Lily noticed the moment when her shallow breathing stopped altogether and her hand dropped on the coverlet. She waited.

"Grandfather," she said quietly. "I think she's gone."

Her grandfather nodded and took Lily's hand. "She was so happy to have seen ya," he said. "All grown up and lovely as a flower, so like her you are in looks. Whenever I see you, you put me in mind of her. I will have that yet to comfort me."

A Special Request

By all accounts the Christmas sermon was very well received. Glowing reports reached Lily, but she didn't care. She was just thankful that due to her profound grief over losing her grandmother that Vicar Rivers had not come calling. She hoped he would lose interest and move on to any of the other eligible young ladies in the area.

Hannah seemed quite taken with him and rather in awe of his sermon-making which she found quite profound. Lily nodded, but she wasn't really listening. She wasn't sure she could bear the loss of her grandmother, after having just lost her parents only a few years past.

She was back in black and haunting her uncle's gardens when it was fine enough to be out. Uncle Nael worried about her and invited Lady Hyde and Hannah over often in hopes of cheering Lily, but nothing seemed to work. Her only comfort seemed to be in riding to see her grandfather, aunt and uncle, and cousins.

She and Luella took to roaming about the fields deep in conversation talking of their grandmother. Luella knew her before her illnesses and told Lily story after story of her kind, gentle ways. It was a help to both of them. When they ventured back indoors, their grandfather or Uncle Percy would take up the story and they would talk for hours.

Lily had missed so much of all their lives, but she had to remind herself how much they had missed of hers. Uncle Nael was dear to her, but seemed to be outside of this grief.

Uncle Nael felt it. He spoke for length about it with Doctor Samuels wondering how to help. He was advised to let Lily's grief run its course. He imagined he was in for a long, melancholy year.

Joshua had become a regular fixture in Uncle Percy's sitting room. Lily found him to be a quiet, but serious young man. Dathan visited too, but not as often. But Joshua was there almost every day and regularly kept his noon meal with the family.

Lily did wonder about it and finally asked Luella about it when they were out for a walk.

"Joshua's been so kind since our Gran's passin'," Luella told her. "When I'm sad or tearful, he just lets me be. He don't try to cajole me out of it like Dathan does. If'n I'm sorrowful, I want to feel it, not be made to feel like I have to cheer up. Why can't I just be sad?"

Lily hugged her cousin. She understood. She often felt Uncle Nael was trying too hard to cheer her, instead of just letting her grieve. It might be too soon, but she was curious. "Does that mean you've decided on Joshua over Dathan?" she asked.

Luella was thoughtful. "I'm beginning to think so, though I hadn't quite put it that way," she replied. "I'm noticing things about Joshua that I hadn't of afore. He seems to know aught about me in a way that Dathan doesn't. Maybe because we're from the some type of people - farming folk. I'm used to working hard and Dathan seems to think a wife of his should just be in the house all the time. I prefer the fields. I think I would suffocate being holed up in a house all the time."

Lily smiled. She was past trying to dictate the direction of her cousin's life. If Joshua would make Luella happy then that's all that mattered. "But would you be leaving here?" Lily suddenly asked.

"Oh no," Luella replied. "Joshua's been hired on as caretaker for the vicarage and Vicar Rivers thinks I could start teaching the young un's their letters, whilst we wait for a teacher to come. Least until my own young un's start coming."

Lily felt almost a feeling of gratitude well up in her for Vicar Rivers. "It was kind of him to think of such a thing," Lily said, wondering what had made him think of Luella. She certainly could read much better now thanks to Lily's influence, and had attempted to teach her brothers and Maggie, but to think of her as a teacher?

"He said the other workers know me and would trust me to teach their young un's more than a stranger," Luella said, answering Lily's thought. "He said it will take some work convincin' the farm workers to 'low the children to spend time schoolin' when they can work in the fields."

"I hadn't thought of that," Lily said. "My parents wanted me to learn. Mother taught me everything herself though. I never went to a school. She probably did that for my father's sake," she said. "Now that I know about his upbringing I realize that he needed to learn along with me."

"I never knowed Uncle William," Luella said, "but Pap says he was the best older brother, standing up for him and keeping t'other boys from teasing him. Seems Pap was a might small for his age 'til he was most grown."

"One summer when I was little, we had a neighbor who could read some. She read to me every day when I could get over there," Luella added. "She was the one that showed me the sounds the letters made. I learned some, but then she left. I'm sure I wud of learned much more if Mam could have taught me, but she didn't know nothin' neither."

"Well, I think you would make a perfect teacher," Lily said. "The children love you and your sweetness makes them want to learn."

"Well, that don't work none on my brothers," Luella laughed. "Reading don't interest them none. But ciphering is something different. Carl knows how to cipher real good."

"Everyone should learn to cipher," Lily agreed. "Especially when you're a worker and need to know if your wages will keep you supplied for the month."

"Let's go back to the house, Lily," Luella suggested. "I'm getting chilled and looks like the sun be setting."

The pair turned toward the house and were met by their grandfather waiting on the porch looking for them.

"There ya' be," Grandfather William said. "I've something I'd like to mention to ya', Luella."

"I'll wait inside for you," Lily said, as she prepared to leave them to their conversation, but their grandfather stopped her.

"This be something for your ears too, if you've a mind to stay," their grandfather said. Lily and Luella settled on the step with him.

"I've been thinkin' on something," Grandfather began. "I'm not long for this world." Both of the girls immediately interrupted him with their protests. "Nah, nah. I know it be true. My Rosana was everything and a piece of me is missing without her. I know ya' mourn her

139

too, but you don't know the love between a man and wife. We been together all this time, I can't bear to be apart from her."

"But we need you too, Grandfather," Lily protested. "I couldn't bear to lose you too!"

"Yar both good girls to be sure," their grandfather said, patting their hands and kissing their cheeks. "Yar a comfort to me. Yar and all the young un's. But I know my time's coming soon and I've a favor to ask of ya'."

"What is it, Grandad?" Luella asked.

"Anything. Of course." was Lily's response.

"It'd make me right happy to see ya' wed, afore I go. You have a willin' n waitin' young man, Luella. If yar decided on him, it would please me to no end to see ya' settled. And if there's any young man you've taken a shine to, Lily, I'd say the same, though I know yar uncle be taking right good care of you."

"Oh, Grandfather!" was all that Lily would say, while Luella kissed her grandfather.

So, just like that Luella was engaged. Joshua was thrilled as he had been kept waiting as it was, and they went to the vicar to arrange everything.

A Wedding

Lily had to admit that Vicar Rivers had quite a stirring way of speaking. The words he had said over her grandmother, the first grave in the church yard, were sweet and hopeful. And the words he was saying now over Luella and Joshua were full of joy for their future.

Of course, she had heard the words before, but he said them as if he meant them, which made Lily feel uncomfortable, though she couldn't imagine why. She was grateful to him, of course, for the attention he paid to her family after Grandmother Rosana's passing.

Vicar Rivers was a frequent visitor at the worker's shack where the family resided, talking for hours with her grandfather and Uncle Percy. But she had no interest in him and was determined to not let his fancy words penetrate her heart.

Besides, she was back in mourning clothes and only changed into the lovely blue dress for today's festivities. There were no flowers for Maggie's hair, given the season, so they made do with ribbons from Lily's wardrobe. Maggie was plenty pleased with the ribbons, so it was no matter.

Lily smiled at her cousin, Luella, as the couple was announced. She was truly happy for her. Uncle Percy took up the fiddle again and led the crowd from the church. The pair passed under arches of pine boughs amid cheers for their happiness. There was no nearby Inn and Uncle Nael's house too far for them to walk to, so only a small group of them returned to Luella's family home to partake of the marriage pie, and as much ale as Uncle Percy could procure to celebrate with them.

When the festivities had ended and all the kisses goodbye were given, Joshua spirited Luella away to the home he had obtained for them. It was small but cozy and Luella assured him she couldn't ask for anything better.

Lily felt sad as she watched Luella stroll away on Joshua's arm. She wondered how often she'd see her cousin now that she was married. They had grown very close and she didn't think that even Hannah and her mother could fill that void although they vowed to try.

Lily hated losing Luella, no matter how happy she was for her. She just didn't want anything to change and Luella marrying Joshua changed everything.

She sighed and gathered her wrap, after kissing her grandfather goodbye and assuring Maggie that she would come for a visit soon.

She returned to the carriage and told James to drive her home.

"Why so sad, Niece?" Uncle Nael asked her as they sat down for the evening meal. "I imagine the wedding was a very festive and pleasant affair, even if they kept it small and intimate."

"It was Uncle," Lily responded, forcing a smile. "There is nothing in the world to be sad about. Luella is married and has been taken off to Joshua's house, Grandmother lays in the church yard, and my own parents will never be there for any special event that may happen in my life."

"Oh Niece, don't take it so hard," Uncle Nael replied. "Though, I have no intention of letting you marry any time soon, I can't keep you here forever. Someday you will find your Joshua. And there may be a measure of sadness that your parents aren't there for the occasion, but there will be joy. You'll see."

Lily was thoughtful. She chided herself for being selfish on her cousin's wedding day. "You're right, Uncle, of course. I will do my best not to miss her so much. It would help if Lady Hyde, Hannah and the boys weren't gone on holiday though, or we could at least have some company."

Uncle Nael hesitated. "I did invite some company over tomorrow. I hope you will be courteous and join us."

Lily was puzzled. Who was coming? Dr. Samuel's was a fixture and dropped in whenever he was nearby. "Vicar Rivers?" she asked.

"Well, I am one of his patrons and it is my responsibility to invite him at the very least to have tea with us. Besides, I enjoy talking to him. I don't usually take with spiritual men, but he doesn't speak as if he is talking to angels, as I have found others in his line of work do. He recognizes the people that he speaks to have the nature of humanity and do not attain perfection. I for one have many vices," Uncle Nael said, smiling.

"Uncle? Why did you give him leave to seek my hand when he came to you?" Lily asked. "I would have thought that you would have asked me first. How is he of any higher rank than Dathan? And you vehemently objected to him."

"And look where it got me," Uncle Nael replied. "You refused to speak to me for weeks and then allowed him to think you cared, just because I said no. I felt that I could not go wrong in giving him leave, but if I had said no, you are so contrary that you'd have married him on the spot just to spite me."

Lily laughed along with her uncle. "I can be quite

stubborn," she sighed. "I will do my best to mend my ways. It was wrong of me to let Dathan think he had any kind of chance with me. I used him to further my own ends. It is no excuse, but I felt hurt at the insult to my father."

"I know, Niece. And I am sorry for it. I feared losing you too soon, but you have proved yourself to be wise and I'm sure you will choose well. However, I am in no hurry. Are you?"

"No, Uncle. I don't think I could bear it. Just when I think my grief has subsided, something happens that causes it to spring up as fresh as it was at first. Perhaps, I'll never marry and stay all of my life here with you. Would that suit you?"

Uncle Nael smiled. "Of course, but suppose I were to marry?" Uncle Nael asked sheepishly, looking at his plate.

"Are you in earnest, Uncle?" Lily asked. "Do you really mean it?"

"I have been thinking on it," Uncle Nael replied. "I even went so far as to speak to Doctor Samuels about it. There is a part of me that is quite afraid of the prospect, having been so long a bachelor. But there is another part of me that thinks it could be quite pleasant. We both enjoy Lady Hyde's company. She could not replace your mother, of course, but she has been a good friend to you. And you and Hannah are close."

"And the boys, Aidan and Aaron?" Lily asked.

"Vicar Rivers has promised to help with the boys," Uncle Nael replied. "He thinks they just need some type of employment to keep them busy. I have asked him to tutor them in their studies and help find an outlet for their energy."

"Have you spoken to Lady Hyde about it?" Lily asked.

Uncle Nael shook his head. "If you are agreeable I plan to do so the moment they return from holiday."

"Of course I'm agreeable, Uncle!" Lily replied.

"Consider carefully, Niece," Uncle Nael cautioned. "It would mean they all would come here to live, even the boys. It would upend our quiet home quite dramatically. And then there is the honeymoon. I plan to take Mrs. Mildenhall away for up to a month and you would be left in charge of the house and the boys."

Lily thought for a moment. "I think, Uncle," she finally replied. "That it may be exactly what I need."

A Proposal

Lily knew that Uncle Nael had settled on proposing marriage to Lady Hyde and she had given her full support, but when a full week after they had returned from holiday and nothing had been said, she began to wonder.

"The truth is, I'm terrified," Uncle Nael confessed.

"You think she'll reject you?" Lily asked, astonished.

"No, I am quite sure I will not be rejected," Uncle Nael smiled. "She has been dropping quite a few hints of late. Dr. Samuels must have mentioned something to her."

"Then what is it, Uncle?"

Uncle Nael sighed. "Everything will change! Again. I am so settled in my ways and there will be children underfoot and a wife! A wife who will try to change me and make me more sociable and there will be parties and she will do worse things to my purse than you have! And my study! What about my study? It is my sanctuary. I can't bear the thought of my sanctuary invaded."

Lily laughed at her uncle's foolishness. "Oh Uncle! You will still be very much king of your own castle. And change is not always bad. Do you regret me?"

"No, of course not," Uncle Nael smiled. "You are the best thing that I could have chosen."

"Oh Uncle," Lily soothed. "Lady Hyde is kind and sensible, Hannah is a dear, and the boys just rambunctious. You have said yourself that Vicar Rivers is to help you with them."

"The truth is Lily, that I am plain afraid. Yes my

house is empty and my legacy left only to you, but it is comfortable and familiar. I'm not sure I could bear it changing all at once."

Lily was thoughtful. "Perhaps we could do it in stages," she suggested. "You and Lady Hyde get married and go on your honeymoon, and Hannah and I will get everything else settled for your return. You'll have a month to settle all the particulars with Lady Hyde and Vicar Rivers for the boys' schooling and activities."

"You are setting forth a very reasonable argument," Uncle Nael replied. "However, when it comes to the point of it, all reason flies out of my head. I make up my mind to ask and then the opportunity comes and I have not done it."

"Well, the family is coming to dinner tomorrow along with Dr. Samuels. Suppose Hannah and I take the boys and Dr. Samuels on a house tour and leave you with Lady Hyde?" Lily suggested. "Would that be agreeable?"

"The words stick in my throat, Niece. I mean to say them and then they don't come out." Uncle Nael sighed again.

"Perhaps we should have to do something unconventional," Lily said, thinking about what that might be.

"You are the most unconventional person I know," Uncle Nael said with a wry smile. "You throw propriety out the window entirely if it suits you. Just like your mother."

"Thank you, Uncle, for the compliment," Lily replied with a smile. "But if it gets the job done then we will do what we must do."

Lily laid out her plan to her uncle. "It will require

Hannah's help and perhaps the boys too. Since this decision affects all of us, we should be a part of it."

Uncle Nael shook his head. "Do you think it would be proper? It doesn't seem to be the way things are usually done."

"The usual way is to ask someone when you are a young pup, and there are no children involved, but we are past that point aren't we?" Lily said slyly. "You are set on Lady Hyde, as am I, and they must be asked if they agree to the proposition."

Uncle Nael assented, although he was sure all manner of things could go wrong. They were all at the dinner table when Lily stood up.

"I have a matter of business to discuss with those of you assembled here," Lily began.

The boys looked at each other. Business? That sounded intriguing.

Hannah smiled her encouragement as Lily continued. "We here at the company of Mildenhall and Niece are looking to expand our enterprise, branch out as it were to other endeavors."

"What is this?" Dr. Samuels asked. "Ladies are now taking up matters of business?"

Lady Hyde kicked him under the table as she was in on the joke. "Please continue, Dear," she said to Lily.

"I have been several years without a mother and am sore in need of one," Lily added. "I have no sister nor brothers to play with nor care for, and Uncle and I have agreed that a partnership is in order."

Dr. Samuels finally caught on and stopped objecting. "Oh, I see," he said.

"Would you, Lady Hyde, be agreeable to joining

our company in the position of mother? And you, Hannah, Aidan and Aaron accept the position of sister and brothers? We have the room and a grand playroom for the boys. That of course, would mean Lady Hyde, that you are also agreeing to be wife to this cantankerous old bachelor."

"But, but, but," Uncle Nael interrupted. "I will still be captain of my own ship! I'll not be usurped in my authority by a wheedling, albeit beautiful, wife."

Lady Hyde cleared her throat. "Well, I believe we will take the matter under advisement. I shall meet with the Board and determine..."

"This is torture!" Uncle Nael interrupted. "I did not think this plan of Lily's to be well advised, but you have been asked and for God's sake, I would like an answer. Please," he added, softening.

Lady Hyde looked at her children. "Hannah?" she asked.

"I vote aye," she said. Lily is already dear to all of us and I also am in want of a father."

"Boys?" Lady Hyde asked. "How do you feel about this venture?"

"You mean we would live in this grand house?" Aidan asked.

"And have all the grounds to play?" added Aaron.

"Yes, and a father and another older sister to obey and listen to. You will study your lessons faithfully and not cause any trouble or else we may have to send you to a boarding school. It is after all the fashionable thing to do among the wealthy." Lady Hyde said sternly.

The boys looked at each other. "We agree," they finally said in unison.

"It is a grand house," Aidan said.

"And the playroom enormous," Aaron added. "Think of the games we shall play."

Lady Hyde nodded. "Then you have your answer, Sir," she said to Uncle Nael. "We are agreeable to joining your corporation."

Uncle Nael laughed at the absurdity of it all. "Will you take a walk with me then, so that we may discuss the terms in private?" he asked Lady Hyde. "I am heartily ashamed to have my niece do my proposing for me."

Lady Hyde agreed and the pair left for a walk in the garden.

"Let's pick our rooms!" Aidan suggested.

"Yes!" added Aaron. "I want the blue one!"

"No, that's mine!" Aidan demanded. "You may take the green."

And so it was agreed. In a month's time the two families would become one. Hannah would take the blue room and the boys would have matching rooms of equal size adjoining the playroom.

The wedding itself was a quiet affair with no one but the families attending. Lady Hyde looked lovely and Uncle Nael as cleaned up as possible for a stuffy old bachelor. Hannah attended for her mother and Dr. Samuels for Uncle Nael. The celebration lasted well past the boys' bedtime, but it was finally over and everyone said goodnight and went to their respective beds.

As they set the happy couple on their way the next morning, Lily couldn't help but feel a twinge of longing. She had wanted a change and now she certainly had it with a new sister and brothers to watch over.

How hard could it be to run a household for a

month? And watch over two rambunctious boys?
But Lily's adventure was just beginning.

Other fiction titles by Sharon L Letson

The Kingdom of Farin Trilogy:
    The Seventh City
    Orion's Song
    A Double-Edged Sword

www.ingramcontent.com/pod-product-compliance
Lightning Source LLC
Chambersburg PA
CBHW061243170626
46809CB00007B/2814